The Saga of Tommy Wade

The Lonely Man

A Novel by
Edward Daley

Order this book online at www.trafford.
com or email orders@trafford.com

Most Trafford titles are also available at major online book retailers.

This novel is a work of fiction. The situations are
fictional. No character is intended to portray any
person or combination of persons living or dead.
Printed in Victoria, BC, Canada.

ISBN: 978-1-4269-2403-3 (sc)
ISBN: 978-1-4269-2406-4 (e)

*Our mission is to efficiently provide the world's finest, most
comprehensive book publishing service, enabling every author to
experience success. To find out how to publish your book, your way,
and have it available worldwide, visit us online at www.trafford.com*

Trafford rev. 1/6/2010

www.trafford.com
North America & international
toll-free: 1 888 232 4444 (USA & Canada)
phone: 250 383 6864 ◆ fax: 812 355 4082

Chapter 1

The sun was just coming up over the hilltop behind him as young Tommy Wade made his way home. It was about 8:00 in the morning. Tommy had gotten up early to go fishing and had made a pretty good catch; he had five good sized cat fish. His ma and pa would be up and wondering where he was. He knew they would be upset. Life on the farm began early and they would have expected him to start milking the cows and doing the rest of the feeding and gathering from the chickens.

Speaking of chickens, they would have already had breakfast. This reminded him that his stomach was beginning to churn from emptiness. He should have grabbed a biscuit before heading out to the lake which was about a mile from the house. But he was in a hurry this morning to catch a fish, something he thought he would never ever get tired of doing. But life, as young Tommy Wade knew it, was about to change forever.

Just as he crested the hill overlooking the house he heard a gunshot; he was about a half mile from home but the sound was clear. It was the sound of a pistol. He knew it would not be his father, because he only had a rifle. He ran the few steps to where he could get a clear look. There in front of his house were three men on horses. The forth man, a man dressed in black, was standing in front of his horse holding its bridle; he had a gun in his hand. In front of the man in black lay his father; face down in the ground. He could hear his mother scream as she grabbed her mouth and ran toward his father. She never made it. The man in black shot her point blank and she reeled backward from the blast falling to her death.

Young Tommy Wade stood there paralyzed from shock and surprise for a moment then began to run down the hill as he started to scream. In his mind was the word "no" but he never got it out. He tripped and fell head long cracking his head on something hard. His world went black.

He didn't know how long he lay there, maybe hours he wasn't sure. When consciousness came to him he slowly began to rise. He could see the blood on the rock in front of him. Then he felt the pounding in his head. He reached up and felt his forehead and felt the thick liquid there. Looking at his hand he saw the blood, he had been knocked out by the rock. Then the realization of the prier events came flooding in.

He remembered his father lying on the ground. The man in black! His mother... Shot!

He looked toward the house and saw what he was afraid to see. There was his father and mother lying very still in front of the house. He hoped upon hope that they weren't dead. He sprang to his feet and began to rush down the hill. The four men were nowhere in sight.

As soon as he got to his father he rolled him over and saw his chest covered with blood from the gunshot. His body began to tremble as he felt the deep hurt and anger. *No, this can't be happening,* he thought. *Why? Why now? Who would do such a thing and for what reason?* Tears were streaming down his face as he went to his mother. She was lying on her back with both arms stretched above her head. Her chest too was covered with blood. "Ma, Ma!" he cried.

He could feel the anger burning deep in his gut. He stood up looking around his fists clenched tightly his teeth grinding as he looked for signs of the four men. *Who were they,* he thought? *Why would they do this? Where did they go?* He could see the tracks leading off away from the farm. His first impulse was to run into the house and get his gun and go after them. But he couldn't leave his parents there, not like this. *What should he do?* He stood there staring at his mother and father. Suddenly, thoughts of this mother and father came flooding into his mind.

He remembered his mother. She was so loving and kind. She always had time to love him and do special things for him on his birthday or holidays. She was always there to support him and nurture him. She read the Bible to him when he was little. She had taught him to read and how to cook eggs and bacon. When he got hurt she was always there to lift him up. She was the school teacher for Chickasha, Oklahoma where they lived and his father was their pastor.

His father had taught him how to farm and to hunt: how to wait for the right shot; and more important, how to fire that rifle. At seventeen years of age he was a good shot with the rifle. He rarely ever needed a second shot. His father was proud of him and who he was. But his father was more than a farmer. He was the town parson. He pastored the church in Chickasha. But he was a different kind of preacher for his day. He was not the hellfire and brimstone type of preacher. He saw God as the God of love: a God who cared for everyone and took care of everyone. *Where was God now,* he thought.

He remembered praying at the altar when he was eight years old and accepting Christ as his savior. His father was very excited about baptizing him in the local fishing hole; the fishing hole where he had just been. Tommy had one problem. He loved to fish when he should be doing the farm chores. He loved to fish more than he loved to hunt and certainly more than he loved to farm, perhaps, even more than he loved God.

He had gone fishing. *Damn* he thought to himself. *How selfish and inconsiderate I was of them both. I was only thinking of myself and my pleasures. Now they're both laying here dead. If I had just stayed at home and done my chores, I might have been able to save them. At least I would know why this happened. Damn me! Damn me!* He thought. Then he paused for a minute as he reassessed the situation. He looked up in the direction the men had gone, *No!* He thought, *Damn them!* He looked around again as his face filled with flame; anger in his eyes turned them almost red.

At the time, he wasn't aware that if he had stayed home, he too, would have been killed. *If it is the last thing I ever do,* he thought, *I will hunt them down; I will find them and kill them all.*

The men who killed his parents were thieves and marauders; a band of renegade Mexican thieves who lived only to rob, kill and take what they wanted. The leader of the gang was Eduardo, a cold and calculating killer of men and rapist of women. Tommy's mother had escaped his hands only because she acted that day without thinking. Eduardo and his men were headed back to Mexico.

When Eduardo came to the farm that day all he and his men wanted was some food and money. He thought it was a simple thing for a man to turn over his money to keep his life, but that fool had rebuked him and told him to leave his home. When he shot the man the woman started toward him and he thought she was waving a gun and he fired on instinct. After she fell to the ground he could see she was unarmed. *That was a waste,* he thought. *She was a pretty woman, and he was in need of a pretty woman's company. Too bad for me, I had fired too quickly.*

Tommy picked up his mother and carried her into the house and laid her on the bed. His father, however, was another story. He outweighed Tommy by at least fifty pounds. There was no way Tommy could get his father into the house and he didn't want to drag him. So he went to the barn and got a tarpaulin they used when they needed to camp outside while hunting. He covered his father with that. He saddled up the old mare and headed for the McGregor's farm. The McGregor's farm was only about 20 miles away; they would help him sort out what he should do next.

The McGregor's were a God fearing family. They were hard working farmers and members of his father's perish. Mr. McGregor was a big Scotsman that everyone respected, not only for his humility, but also for of his size. He was indeed a mountain of a man about six foot five and weighed about three hundred pounds. His wife Joelle was completely different. She was a small woman with beautiful features and often turned heads even when she wore a bonnet. She was a soft spoken woman but William McGregor often moved to her bidding. They had two children Billy the son was fifteen and Molly their daughter was thirteen. Molly took after her mother in looks and features. She was a pretty girl and always had a crush on Tommy. However, Tommy never paid any attention to her because she was too young. Billy was like his father; he was already a big boy at fifteen with broad shoulders and a height of six foot.

Tommy couldn't help but break into tears as he rode onto the McGregor's farm. Mr. McGregor, seeing him ride up on the mare in the middle of the day, knew something was wrong. He was in the field plowing and immediately stopped what he was doing and headed for the house.

Tommy rode up to the house and jumped off of the horse. He was greeted my Mrs. McGregor. "Tommy," she said, "What are you doin ridin in such a hurry; is something wrong"?

"My ma and pa," Tommy paused for a breath as his eyes burst with tears. "They've both been killed, murdered. They've been shot by four men, I never saw before. I had to leave them at the house. I didn't know what to do."

"Oh! My God," said Mrs. McGregor, as she rushed to take him into her arms. "Are you sure boy?"

"Yes... I'm sure. They're both dead... I carried my ma into the house but my pa's layin out in the yard. I don't know what to do." He sobbed. "I couldn't pick up pa, he was too heavy."

Mr. McGregor heard what was being said as he joined the group. He turned and looked at Billy who had just gotten there too. "Billy," he said. "Go hook up the buckboard and be quick about it son."

Billy took off for the barn to do what he was told. He couldn't believe his ears. *Someone had killed Tommy's ma and pa*, he thought, as he hurried to get the buckboard. *Who would do such a thing?"*

Molly who had been with her mother stood there in disbelief. As she looked at her mother consoling Tommy she too wanted to hug him but she couldn't. *It wouldn't be proper*, she thought, *and Tommy might take offense.* She stood there, her heart breaking, trembling as tears fell from her eyes. She was bound by the customs but she so desperately wanted to hold Tommy and help him. All she could do was stand there and watch as she cried from her broken heart.

"Tommy," said Mr. McGregor. "You said you saw who did this?"

Tommy turned to face Mr. McGregor breaking loose from Joelle's embrace. "Yes sir, I saw them, but I never saw them before." He said. "When I saw them from the hilltop... I had gone fishing that morning, and was just gettin home. Pa was already dead and I saw the man in black shoot my ma in the chest. I couldn't do anything, I was too far away. I dropped my fish and started to run, but I tripped on something and fell. I got knocked out. When I came too, they were gone. Then I ran to the house, but I was too late to help. After I carried my ma into the house, I covered up pa and came straight over here. I would have carried my pa in the house, but he was too heavy."

"Lord... I'm sorry Tommy," said Mr. McGregor, "Your folks were good people, but if you can describe the men to the sheriff, I'm sure he'll be able to get them."

Tommy's anger returned as he felt his body go stiff. "I guess," he said. He didn't want anyone to get them. He wanted to kill them the same way they had killed his ma and pa. Tommy stopped crying. His anger had overwhelmed him. All he felt was fury. His whole body was trembling and crying out for revenge. He remembered in one of his father's sermons he said,

"The Bible says that, 'vengeance is mine, I will repay,' saith the Lord..." *Not this time*, he thought. *This time I'll repay.*

Billy came driving up in the buckboard and they all piled in and headed for Tommy's house.

Chapter 2

Two months had passed. Tommy's parents were laid to rest. The McGregor's had wanted him to stay with them, but he couldn't. If the truth be known, he couldn't stand the praying anymore, and they were very religious. Plus, he was aware of Molly's feelings for him and he didn't want to lead her on. They had always played together when they were younger, and he liked her, but they were older now and things were different. He had become a man, but he thought of her as a child. He couldn't understand what a thirteen year old girl would see in a man like him. He didn't understand girls, or women, at all.

The bank had settled with him for the farm since he could no longer take care of it himself. What little money was left he deposited in the bank. At least he had a few hundred dollars.

He had gotten a job in the livery stable taking care of the horses and cleaning up after them. It also came with a room in the barn. It wasn't the best smelling place to live, but he didn't have to pay any rent. Mr. Burly, or just Burly as people called him, was the owner of the stable. He was a big guy like his name, but he was kind and fair with everyone, including Tommy.

In these past few months, Tommy had thought of nothing else other than finding the men who had killed his folks. The sheriff had mounted a posse but was unable to locate any of the killers. Tommy's only thought was how could he find them? *It was time*, he thought. He headed toward Jennings General Store.

"Hello, Mr. Jennings," said Tommy to the owner of the store.

"Hi, Tommy, what can I do for you today?"

"Well, Mr. Jennings, I thought I would like to purchase a handgun."

"A handgun... Why in the world would you want to carry around a handgun?"

"Well," said Tommy. "I really don't have a whole lot to do anymore since I no longer have a farm to tend to. I thought I would get in a little target practice, maybe get ready for the turkey shoot coming up."

"That might not be a bad idea, Tommy. Your father told me that you were a crack shot with a rifle. But if that's true why worry about a handgun?"

"Well, let's just say, that I win the Turkey Shoot with the rifle and with the handgun too. What do you think?"

"I guess you have a point," said Mr. Jennings. "What kind of gun are you lookin for?"

"I want one of those with the long barrel." Tommy thought that if he was good with the rifle he would be good with a longer barreled pistol.

"I think what you mean is a Colt 45." Mr. Jennings opened the case and pulled out a long barreled Walker Colt 45. He handed it to Tommy.

Tommy had never held a pistol before and he really didn't know what to do with it. *How do you know if a gun is right for you or not*, he thought? He had to look like he knew what he was doing, so he held it up and looked at it and then pointed it at the wall. His mind went back to the day when the man in black had pointed his gun at his mother and pulled the trigger. He could see his mother flying backwards. Then he pictured himself shooting the man in the chest and watching him as he flew backward. "How much is this," he asked?

"Well, that's a pretty expensive one there. I do have cheaper ones but they're not a Walker Colt 45. The Walker is the top of the line these days. I'd have to have twenty dollars for that one."

"Twenty dollars is a lot of money," said Tommy. He thought about it for awhile then decided. "Well... okay, Mr. Jennings, and I'll take two boxes of the cap's and black powder."

"There you go son," said Mr. Jennings as he placed the loads on the counter, "With the black powder and caps that will be twenty two dollars." Tommy started to get the money out of his pocket when Mr. Jennings asked, "How about a nice holster to go with it?"

"No, holster for now. Let me see how hard it is to fire this thing. I might be selling it back to you," he smiled.

Tommy didn't know if he could master the handgun or not. If it was too hard then he would stick with the rifle. He had one thought in mind. He was about to start planning for his future and the death of the man in black. Tommy paid for the gun and ammunition and then put the gun in his belt.

"Tommy," said Mr. Jennings, "you might let me put that in a bag for you. You don't want to upset people as they see you walking around town with a gun in your belt. What would they think?"

"Why would people think any different if they saw me carrying it in my belt than if I carried it in a holster?"

"Tommy my boy, if people carry a gun in there belt it means they intend to use it; however, many men carry a gun in a holster in case they need to use it. Do you understand the difference?"

Tommy thought about his words for a moment. "Of course, you're right Mr. Jennings. I guess, I wasn't thinking." He handed the gun back to Mr. Jennings as he looked once again at the holsters.

Mr. Jennings put the gun and ammunition in a bag and handed it to him. Tommy headed back to his room at the stable. On his way he stopped by the sheriff's office.

"Hi, Sheriff," said Tommy as he entered the sheriff's office.

"Hi, Tommy, what can I do for you?"

"I was wondering," he continued, "if you have gotten any information about that gang that killed my parents?"

"Not much I'm afraid," said the sheriff. "We heard there is a gang of Mexicans that's lead by a man named Eduardo. But we don't know if he's the man who killed your parents or not. He is a notorious outlaw and he was in this area about the time, but we just don't have all of the evidence we need to arrest him. For that matter, we're not really sure where he is, he could be back in Mexico by now."

"If he's as notorious as you say, why don't you have a picture of him or something?"

"Pictures are easier to talk about than to get. The best we could hope for is an artist's sketch. The problem is that anyone that has ever gotten close to this gang either ends up dead or won't talk because they're afraid for their lives. Either way, we don't have a picture."

"Well, I was wondering Sheriff if you might need another deputy?" Tommy asked.

"We certainly could use someone else that's for sure. But the city won't cough up any more money to pay for one. And if you're thinking about yourself, I think you're a little young and green behind the ears for law enforcement. You see son, you not only have to enforce the law but you have to know what the law says. I don't think you're educated in that area yet."

Tommy was embarrassed by the sheriff's put down. "Oh, I didn't mean me. I know I'm too young, and I don't know anything about the law. But, I do know it is wrong to steal and to kill. I just thought you might need some more help to catch those men, that's all."

"I understand. And don't you worry any about those desperados we will get them eventually. They all end up in the same place. You're a good boy Tommy. You continue to keep your nose clean and stay out of trouble and we'll take care of those men. Okay?"

"Yeah, and thanks sheriff for the information. I'll be waiting to hear some good news."

As Tommy left the sheriff's office he knew better than to depend on him to get the killers. A sheriff could only go so far out of town before he crossed another county line; he would have no jurisdiction there. Tommy needed to go after them himself. But first he needed to learn how to use a handgun. He knew in a fist fight he would be no match against a professional but he could be faster and better than anyone else with a gun. That was the equalizer. Age didn't matter to a bullet it went where it was sent.

For the next few months Tommy kept to himself. He bought himself a horse and would go out of town to practice firing the gun. He had gotten much better but he had a long way to go. The gun kept getting hung up on his cloths or on the holster he had recently bought. He knew he didn't need to be the fastest gun, but he did need to get it out fast enough. He would keep practicing. If he had learned anything in his young life, it was that practice makes perfect. His father had said it enough, and it proved to be true concerning the rifle. He could hit just about anything he wanted to, and he was getting better with the pistol all the time.

One day, he was grooming a mare when Mr. McGregor walked in. "Hi Tommy," he said. "I wanted to give you this telegram that I received from your uncle Jake. I sent him a letter months ago right after your parents died. I had to send it to the last address I had for him. I finally received this telegram from him today. He says in here that he was sorry to hear about his brother's death and that he was on his way here to see you."

As Tommy reached for the telegram he was reminded that uncle Jake was the black sheep of the family. His ma and pa never spoke much about him other than telling him that Jake went to prison for killing a man. He was a wonderer. He never held a job longer than to get enough money to move on. His dad thought he was a bum, a saddle tramp. He certainly wasn't someone his father would want him to be around. But he was family. It would be good to see him if only briefly. As best he could remember he looked a lot like his father, but then, he hadn't seen him since he was six or seven years old. And as far as he knew his folks had not heard from him. "Thanks, Mr. McGregor," Tommy said as he opened the telegram to read. It was short.

Hi William,
Sorry to hear about Tom and Martha.
The kid must be taking it hard.
I thank you for taking care of him.
Tell him I'm on my way.
I'll be there.
Jake

Tears welled up in Tommy's eyes. *Family,* he thought. He couldn't wait to see him. He wondered what he looked like now and what kind of a man he was. But at the same time it really didn't matter, he was family.

Tommy looked at Mr. McGregor. "Thank you! I forgot all about my uncle. I haven't seen him, or heard anything about him in years."

"Now don't get your hopes up too high boy. As best I can remember, he never stayed anywhere very long. And he and your pa were not on the best of terms. I don't know a whole lot about that, nor do I know your uncle that well. I only met him a few times, and your pa never talked too much about him, other than to say he was a drifter."

"I don't remember anything about him," Tommy said. "Ma and pa wouldn't talk about him."

"I know boy. That's what I mean," said Mr. McGregor. "So don't get your hopes up."

Just then Molly walked into the barn behind her pa. "Dad," she said. "Ma's ready to go. She sent me to fetch you!"

Tommy was stunned when he saw her. It had only been about six month and he knew she had turned fourteen. But he wasn't prepared for how much a girl can change in six months. She was really pretty and something about her really glowed. Tommy was speechless; he just stood there staring at her. *My,* he thought, *she sure is pretty. If she wasn't so young, I might begin to change my mind about her.*

"Hi Tommy," she said. "How are you doing these days? We haven't seen much of you. I heard you have a horse. You ought to stop by the house for supper sometime?"

Tommy's lips began to move, "I... I... well I do have a horse and it might be good to get some home cookin now and then." His voice had come back to him. He would have to remember to keep that invitation open.

"Fine, my boy," said Mr. McGregor. "You just stop by anytime. You know what time we eat supper and you're always welcome, you know we consider you part of the family."

Tommy just stood there nodding but he never took his eyes off of Molly. She just looked at him with that silly little smile he remembered; however, somehow it didn't seem so silly anymore. As a matter of fact, it seemed real warm and friendly. Tommy could feel his heart stepping up a pace as he watched them turn and walk away. Molly took a few steps, as she swayed her hips, and then turned to look over her shoulder.

Tommy was still watching them and then she realized; he was watching her. She smiled at him again. Slowly she saw the smile come onto his face. *Yes!* She thought. *Yes!*

Chapter 3

It was only a few weeks later. Tommy was returning to the stable from Jennings General Store when he noticed the black stallion tied at the rail. *Wow!* Tommy thought. *That's an incredible horse. The shiniest strongest looking stallion I've ever seen. I wonder who owns it; I've never seen anything like it before.* As he walked into the barn he saw a big strong looking man talking to Mr. Burly. As the man turned around to face Tommy; his mouth fell open in shock and surprise. *It's my pa,* Tommy thought. *But it can't be, I was there when they laid him to rest.*

"Sorry boy. I guess your father never told you, I was his twin brother. I'm Jake."

Tommy was stunned. "His twin brother... no, he never said." Tommy didn't know what to say or how to react. "So... you're Uncle Jake?"

"That's right boy. I'm sorry to hear about your ma and pa. I thought I'd get here as quick as I could and see if there's anything I can do."

"Thanks," said Tommy. "But there's nothin anyone can do now."

"I don't mean for your ma and pa boy, I mean for you."

"For me, what can you do for me?"

"That's my question boy."

"I don't know. I have a job here at the livery stable working for Mr. Burly. I also have a room over there." He pointed. "What else is there?"

"Well, I have a lot of questions. We need to go somewhere and talk. Are you hungry boy? He looked at Tommy. He was waiting for an answer, but when he didn't speak he said, "how about that little diner down the street?"

"I recon," said Tommy. "Is it all right with you Mr. Burly if I take a lunch break now?"

"Sure Tommy," said Burly. "There's not much happening today and your uncle just got into town; why don't you take the rest of the day off. If I need you I can find you. Have a good meetin with your uncle."

"Thanks," said Tommy. As they walked toward the diner, Tommy began to size-up his uncle. He was big in the shoulders and chest like his dad and was almost identical to him in looks and features; but there was a hardness about him that made him look mean. The stern look on his face made you feel a little uneasy. It was like not knowing what to make of him or what might set him off. Tommy was glad to see him but he was also uncomfortable around him.

Jake too was thinking about the boy as they walked to the diner. He wasn't so much a kid anymore. *Hell*, he thought. *He's almost as big as me.* Farm life had made the boy strong and he had his mother's good looks. He was wondering what he could do to help him. As a matter of fact, he had been thinking about that ever since he heard of his brother's death. He was planning on going after the men who killed Tommy's mother and father, but he would have to make sure Tommy was okay first.

After they ordered lunch at the diner, Jake began to question Tommy about his parents. He found out about the four Mexicans and the one dressed in black that had pulled the trigger. He learned that the sheriff and his posse had only been gone about two weeks and returned empty handed. *Hell*, he thought. *It takes months to catch a desperado sometime years; not weeks.* He was going to talk to the sheriff.

"It looks to me boy, like the sheriff ain't doin much. I think I'll go have a talk with him."

"You can talk to him if you want, but you won't find out much except they don't know where they are."

"That might be," said Jake. "What're you doin now, besides workin at the stable? What're you plannin on doin with your life?"

"I don't know right now Uncle Jake," said Tommy. "All I can think about is gettin those guys who killed my parents."

What are you thinkin about doin?"

"It makes me angry to think they're out there doing to others like they did to my folks. I want to do something about it."

"What do you want to do about it?" Jake said. "What are you thinkin, I know your thinkin something."

Anger welled up in Tommy again as he thought about those men, and especially the one in black. "I'm gonna kill them. I'm gonna kill em all."

"And how do you plan on doin that boy?"

"I'm workin on it, and quit calling me boy. I haven't been a boy since ma and pa died."

"Fair enough," said Jake. "But how do you plan on killin these men?"

"Pa taught me how to use a rifle, and I bought a handgun, I been practicing with. I can hit almost anything I see. When I'm ready, I'll head out."

"Sounds like you got a plan, bo... Tommy. But in order to go after these men you have to be better than good. You have to be the best. You can't hit your target 'almost every time,' to be good; you have to hit your target 'every time.' How long do you think it'll take you to get that good?"

Tommy looked at him with an angry expression on his face, "it'll take just as long as it takes."

"Whoa! You're a feisty little cuss aren't you," said Jake.

"Maybe," replied Tommy. "But I am not so little, in case you haven't noticed."

"All right, you're not a boy and you're not a kid, I get that. But watch your tone with me boy, I am bigger than you, and I'm sure I could box your ears a little if I had to. However, I don't intend to do that. As I said before, I am here to help you. As a matter of fact, I was planning on goin after those guys myself. But I was plannin on doin it alone."

"You're going after them?"

"That's what I said. But I was plannin on doin it alone. But now you got me curious. Why don't we take a ride out of town so you can show me what you can do with that gun?"

All of a sudden Tommy was excited, almost overcome with emotion. His uncle was planning on going after those guys, and now was considering on taking him.

They went back to the livery stable, and got their horses, and rode out of town. Neither man spoke on the trail. Both men were thinking over the situation. Tommy was hoping his uncle would take him along. His uncle seemed rugged enough and knew something about violence he was sure, but how much experience did he have in hunting down a bad man.

Jake was thinking about the boy. *Tommy is determined to get the people that killed his parents. I commended him for that; that's what I would have done, and that's what I intend to do. But how much did this kid have to learn? Being determined to get the people you are after is one thing, but not getting killed in the process is another. It would probably take months, maybe even years, to find these guys. It may be possible to teach this boy how to survive.* First however, he would have to see what he had learned on his own, and then how teachable he was.

They came to a clearing on the back side of a ridge. Both men dismounted and Jake set up some targets. "Okay boy, let's see what you can do with that rifle."

Tommy looked at his uncle and said, "Uncle Jake, I wish you would quit calling me a boy. I don't feel like a boy anymore. And it's really rilin me up."

"I'll tell you what 'son,' you prove to me you're a man and I'll quit calling you a boy."

Son! The word caught him by surprise. He felt overcome with hurt and pain as it brought back memories of his father. Tears welled up once again in his eyes as he stood looking at his uncle. *Pa*, he thought to himself. *I miss you so bad.* He gritted his teeth and pointed the rifle from a standing position and began to fire. He hit four out of ten targets. He was nervous. "Not too bad," he said. "This is from standing and I am nervous, but I still got four of them."

"Four of them and you still have six of them shooting at you. How can you thank that wasn't bad." With that Jake pulled his rifle from the holster on his horse, turned and fired rapidly as he cocked the lever on his Winchester, all targets were gone.

Tommy stood there in disbelief. He had never witnessed anything like that before. Jake quickly drew his side arm and turned while fanning his 44 he quickly blew the needles off the side of a cactus that was about twenty-five feet away. He spun the 44, four or five times, and slid it back into the holster. He turned and looked at Tommy, then pulled the 44 back out of the holster and began to reload it. Spinning the gun and slipping it back in the holster was just for show, but you never left an unloaded gun in your holster.

The boy stood there looking at him in shock. "Tommy," Jake said. "What chance would you have against me, no matter how good you think you are, if I wanted to draw down on you right now?"

The boy shook his head from side to side. "None at all, I suppose."

"You suppose right, son. And I'm by no means the fastest gun in the west. But I have learned a few tricks about how to survive and if you want to go with me and get those people responsible for your ma and pa's death, then you'll have to learn too. I'll teach you. But the first lesson you need to learn is that it doesn't matter what I call you or anyone else calls you; it's what you think of yourself that matters. If you prove yourself to be honorable, respectable and trustworthy you will earn a name for yourself. And other people will call you by that name. Thank about this. What did people say about your pa or your ma? Did you ever hear anyone say anything bad about them? I know you didn't, because they earned the name they were called. As for me, I guess, I've earned the name I've been called too."

Tommy just stood there with his mouth open. He never figured his uncle was a fast gun, nor did he figure he had this much wisdom. He sounded a lot like his father the preacher. He was wondering how much alike they really were. However, it really didn't matter. His uncle was offering to teach him how to draw, aim and fire like a breeze; and he was ready to learn. "Okay," said Tommy. "When do we start?"

"No time like the present," he said. "But the first thing tomorrow we need to get you another hip iron. That Colt 45 is good if you want to shoot someone at the other end of town, or if you're chasing someone on a horse, but not for close fightin. That barrel's too long, and it's too hard to get out of that holster quickly. You can keep it because it is a good gun, but we need to get you another one with a shorter barrel. For now though, slip my gun in that holster and see if it doesn't come out easier."

Tommy took his gun and tried it a few time. He was right it did come out easier. He was already twice as fast as he was before. *But*, thought Tommy, *how was his uncle able to fire from his hip and hit those needles?*

No one could learn everything in one day, however, they did spend the rest of the day learning how to aim and fire. Tommy was a quick study and Jake was impressed. The boy could shoot and was already improving. By the end of that afternoon Tommy was hitting eight out of ten targets and that was drawing his gun. *Not bad for an afternoon's work*, thought Jake.

Tommy told his uncle that he had an open invitation to the McGregor's for supper, and he was sure that they would want to see him. Since it was almost supper time they headed for the McGregor's farm.

On the way to the McGregor's, Jake and Tommy went through town; they stopped there at Jennings General Store. Jake picked up and paid for Tommy a

Smith & Wesson 44 along with another holster. The Smith & Wesson 44 was a five chamber cartridge firing pistol that was much quicker to load than the Colt 45 with ball and caps. The gun belt that Tommy had bought for the Walker Colt 45 was the kind that would easily slide through a holster. Jake placed a holster on each side so that the Colt 45 was on Tommy's left hand side with the handle pointing to the front. In this position it could be drawn with the right hand to fire. Tommy could use this weapon for when he didn't need to draw fast.

The 44 he put on Tommy's right side for fast draw. The Smith & Wesson 44 was a unique weapon in itself. It had a stock that attached to the end of the pistol handle making it a short rifle. On the stock was an adjustable sight so that one could take aim while holding the stock against their shoulder. The stock would be carried in Tommy's saddle bag. As for the 44 and 45, Tommy would have to get use to carrying the weight of the guns. In time, he could decide which one he really wanted to use.

As for him, Jake carried two 44's, he believed if he had to draw another time it would already be too late, but one should always be prepared for the unexpected. As for Tommy, he was young and needed to learn and develop his own beliefs. Jake was hoping that throughout this ordeal he would be able to protect him, or even change his mind. The boy wasn't a killer, but once a man tasted of killing, it became much easier to take a life.

Chapter 4

Mr. and Mrs. McGregor were happy to see Jake; it had been a long time. They did the usual greetings and small talk, but Jake was aware that they felt uncomfortable with him there. As they sat around the dinner table they continued their conversation.

"Tell me Jake," said Mr. McGregor. "The last time we heard from you was from prison. You didn't go into any details about why you were there and that's okay, it's your business. But what have you been doing since you got out?"

"Well, a man has to make a living. I make mine by herding cattle, workin a ranch, or sometimes as a deputized lawman. I guess, I should add, sometimes I just go after the bad man by myself."

"You mean like a bounty hunter?" asked Tommy.

"Yeah, something like that, it got me into trouble once. That's how I landed in prison for five years. The man I was after had a lot of friends that testified that I provoked him into drawing, and he had no choice. I could have been hung, but the jury had trouble believing everything that was said. That was good for me. Course, there's two sides to every story, they just didn't believe mine."

"You mean," said Mr. McGregor, "you were after that man because he was wanted; there was a reward out for him?"

"Yeah, that's what I mean. That's why I said some of the jury couldn't believe what they were hearing."

Tommy couldn't help but wonder so he asked the question that the others were thinking. "How many men have you shot or killed?"

"A few," said Jake. "But, I never killed a man that wasn't trying to kill me. If you live by the gun you're going to end up killing someone, or getting yourself killed. It is not a life that anyone should choose; but once you kill someone and the word gets out then their family comes looking for you. From then on you have no choice unless you can find somewhere to live where no one knows who you are." He paused for a moment and looked around the table. "That's why you haven't heard from me, and that's why I don't come around family. It is too dangerous if I stay in one place too long," he said, "especially for the family."

Tommy was thinking over what his uncle was saying. *So, that's why he's so good with a gun. He has to stay ready at all times to defend himself. That's not a life, I would* want to live. But, on the other hand, I have business to tend to, and Uncle Jake said he was going to take me with him. I wonder if I could learn to be as good with a gun as he is.

As Tommy continued to think about what his uncle was saying, he couldn't help but notice that Molly had been watching him from across the table. His sideway glances at her created a smile on her pretty face. *Damn*, he thought. *She sure is a pretty girl. If she wasn't so much younger than me, things might be different between us.* It was true she stirred up some really deep feelings in him that he'd like to explore. But, what would her ma and pa say to him if they knew what he was thinking. For that matter what would her pa do to him? *Man*, he thought, *I have to quit thinking about her.* But he was beginning to realize that was easier said than done.

Mr. McGregor broke the silence. "Jake, are you planning on going after the men that killed your brother?"

"You bet your sweet ..." he caught himself as he quickly looked around the room, "behind I am. It doesn't seem like the sheriff is interested, and Tommy is determined to go after them too. So if I don't go, he'll likely go alone."

"Is that true?" Mr. McGregor said as he turned to face Tommy.

"Yes," said Tommy. "They killed my folks, and I intend to kill them."

Mr. McGregor looked at Tommy in surprise, "haven't you heard a word that your uncle has said. If you live by the gun you will die by the gun. You had to have heard your father say that many times; and you're too young to go gallivanting around the country looking for these men. These men are dangerous, and you're only going to get yourself killed. I had hopes that you might decide to stay here and work the farm with me. And you know, Molly is just dying to see that happen." He turned and looked at his daughter as he said that.

Both Tommy and Molly were caught by surprise. They quickly, as on cue, turned to face each other with their mouths open, but they had no response. Tommy thought, *There it is. He said it. He knows that we have feelings for each other; I mean she has feelings for me?* His heart was beating so fast he thought his chest would explode.

Molly was thinking the same thoughts, but she reacted in a little different way. Her face turned red from embarrassment, but her heart was skipping beats as it pounding rapidly. Her father had said what she couldn't express. It was out there now. What would Tommy do?

Tommy felt his face getting warm, and he quickly turned to look at Mr. McGregor: then at Jake, then he glanced around the table to look at the others, Mrs. McGregor, and Molly's brother Billy. No one said anything for awhile as they looked from one to another.

Finally, Mr. McGregor spoke, "Come on Tommy, and the rest of you. The only one that should be surprised is Jake, because he hasn't been around. That girl's been sweet on Tommy near all her life."

Mrs. McGregor spoke up, "Even so, William, you needn't embarrass her, or Tommy that way. As best I can remember, you were a little slow on the take yourself. I practically had to hog tie you to get your attention."

It was Mr. McGregor's turn to be at a loss for words, as he took in what his wife was saying.

"If you all excuse me," Molly said. "I think I'll take a walk." With that she stood up pushing her chair back so fast that it almost fell over. She turned and walked out the door without another word.

Tommy turned and looked at Jake who was tilting his head and nodding to the right indicating that he should follow her. Tommy glanced around the room, and saw that they were all looking at him, to see what he would do. Embarrassed and nervous, he stood up, pushed his chair back, and said, "Excuse me," and followed Molly out the door.

He couldn't see the reaction of the others as he walked out the door, but they were looking at each other as they smiled in agreement. Once outside, he saw Molly sitting on the porch swing. She was looking at him. He didn't know what to say, but he knew he had to say something. He slowly walked over to the swing and said to her. "You don't mind if I sit here, do you?"

"No," she said and then fell silent. But inside she was a case of nerves. She felt so excited to be sitting next to him and knowing that it was out in the open. *What will he do now?* She was thinking. She was waiting and hoping that somehow she could touch him. Maybe they could hold hands. She would like that. But she couldn't move: she seemed to be frozen in place.

Tommy had sat down on the opposite side of the swing away from her. There was at least room for one other person to sit between them. He wanted to say something, but couldn't think of anything to say. His heart was beating hard, and he was sure she could see his chest moving. He was afraid to speak because he was afraid no words would come out. *God,* he thought, *what should I do now?*

After a few more minutes of silence, it was Molly who spoke first. "Pa shouldn't have said that. It was mean and embarrassing." She paused for a minute, and looked down at her hands, then continued, "If it offended you, I'm sorry. But, what he said was true; I guess, you knew how I felt." She glanced over at him but he was looking away. "Truth is, I really like you, and you know we've always been friends." No reaction. "I know you like me, and it's all right if you don't like me the way I like you." She paused again and bit her lip, "I'll understand."

Tommy slowly turned to look at her as the glow of light from the window caught her face at just right angle. *Wow,* he thought. *She sure is pretty, and there's that glow on her face again.* His heart was still beating fast, but he knew he had to be in control; after all, he was the older of the two. "Molly," he said, "You're a sweet girl, but you're really too young for me. I'm a grown man, and men don't take a fancy to young girls; it just isn't right." He believed what he said was true, but that wasn't what he really felt. What he really felt, was like taking her up in his arms and kissing her. He wanted to say the hell with right and wrong. He had a strong compelling urge to grab her and crush her to him. *Gosh*, he thought. *I never felt this way before.* But he couldn't act on his feeling. He was a man, and men controlled their feelings.

Molly was embarrassed and hurt she thought to herself, *A girl! He thinks I'm a girl! Doesn't he have eyes? Can't he see I have breast? Girls don't have breasts. A woman's got breast. And a woman's got needs. And I got needs. I can feel them all right, and they ain't girl's needs. There woman's needs.* She jumped up from the swing and her anger exploded from her lips.

"Tommy Wade, I've known you forever and you've never said anything to me that was so mean. You think you're a man and I'm a girl. Look at me and tell me I'm a girl. Girls don't have a bosom, and girls don't have feelin's like I got. I might be young, but so are you. So don't be tellin me about men, and women, or girls. It's something you evidently don't know anything about." With that she stormed back into the house slamming the door behind her. Everyone turned to look at her as she passed the table where they were sitting, but she said nothing as she headed for her room.

Tommy sat there in shock; he was hurting and trembling from her sharp words. *I didn't intend to hurt her,* he thought. *And now, look what I went and done.* Then the words that she said came flooding in. *Bosom... did she say bosom? And needs, a woman's got needs. What did she* mean by that, a woman's got needs? I guess she's right, maybe I don't understand women. But breasts, yeah breast, he never saw a woman's breast, but he did have some curiosity about them. He felt strange thinking about that part of a woman. But he had noticed her for sure, she did have a bosom. Now that he was thinking about it, that's what had caught his eye at the stable. He had noticed she had breast. Do women grow breasts in six months? *Maybe*, he thought, *she is more of a woman now since she's got breasts. And I wonder what she meant by needs?* He knew he had to quit thinking about what she said. It wasn't right to think of a woman like that. He could feel something deep in his stomach that troubled him. *Woman... did he say woman?* What would his father the preacher tell him to do?

"*Pa*, he said to himself, as he looked up at the stars in the sky, *what should I do now? I've really hurt the only friend I've ever had. I guess, I need to quit treating her like a kid. Wow, does that mean I should start treating her like a woman.*"

Tommy was deeply troubled and lost in thought when he heard the door open and saw Jake come out looking for him. "Boy, what did you do to that little filly?" Jake said.

"I told you to quit calling me a boy, and I don't think it's any of your business."

"And I told you," Jake said, "when you start acting like a man then I'll start treating you like one. Now, what did you say to the little filly?"

"What you just called her is what I called her, and she just blew up."

"You mean, you called her a filly?"

"No! I didn't call her a filly," said Tommy, "I said she was a girl, and I can't believe she got so hot about that. She just exploded. Man she told me off big time. I never saw that side of her afore."

"Oh!"Said Jake, "Son, you never call a young woman a girl. If you do, well I don't need to tell you what will happen, you just saw for yourself."

"What should I do?"

"I don't think there's much you can do for now. We need to be burnin leather tomorrow early. But, if you get a chance before we leave, and she still wants to talk to you, you might try to tell her you're sorry."

"Yeah, I guess you're right," said Tommy. He surly did feel bad, and he was hoping he would get a chance to talk to her in the morning. But he couldn't stop thinking about what she said about breasts and feelings. He wondered if she was having the same feelings that he was having, those feelings about wanting to hold her. Was she feeling that way too? Is that what she meant? He wondered.

Mr. and Mrs. McGregor didn't say anything as Tommy and Jake walked back into the room. They already had a pretty good idea about what had happened. They all turned in for the night. Tomorrow would be here soon enough. And it was.

Chapter 5

I t started out to be a rather cold breakfast that morning, at least for conversation. They gathered around the table, but other than greeting each other "good morning," little was said. Molly was silent. She glanced at Tommy several times, but she said nothing as she ate. She was still angry from last night; Tommy really hurt her when he had called her a girl. She may only be fourteen years old, but she had the body and feelings like a woman, and she knew she was one. She couldn't believe she had said those things to Tommy about her breasts and having women's feelings. Women didn't talk that way; at least she had never heard her mother say anything like that. She had been up most of the night trying to calm down and was still angry this morning. *Where'd those words come from?* She thought. *I would never say anything like that out loud. God, I am so embarrassed and ashamed. How can I face Tommy at breakfast? Darn him anyway. It serves him right; he shouldn't have said I was a girl.*

Tommy too had not gotten much sleep last night. He lay awake thinking about how much he had hurt her, and he could see this morning that she was still very much upset. He knew that he and Jake would have to leave after breakfast, and he was wondering if he would get a chance to talk to her before they left.

Mrs. McGregor was the first to speak, "You know, this is a real sad state that we're in; it reminds me of being at a funeral or something. Tommy and Jake are going to be riding out shortly, and I don't know when we might see them again. As a matter of fact, truth be told, they might not come back. When you go looking for trouble sometimes it finds you before you can find it. I think we ought to be acting like we care about one another. Especially you Molly and Tommy! You've been friends as long as you've known each other. You can't let some little riff like what happened last night come between the two of you. You need to talk it out; and you need to talk it out, now." Her voice was very firm and she kept looking from one to the other as she spoke. She was hoping that she could get them to talk to each other.

Molly and Tommy knew she was right, but neither of them knew how to break the ice. They glanced at each other, but said nothing. Molly was still hurting from last night and wanted an apology. Tommy would apologize if he could get the chance, but he didn't know how to do that without looking foolish. It was Mr. McGregor that gave him the chance.

"I think Ma's right," said Mr. McGregor. "You two need to take a walk, and spend some time together, and sort this thing out." Molly and Tommy looked at each other, but neither of them moved. "Come on you two," said Mr. McGregor. "Get up and take a walk, and don't you two come back until this whole thing is settled; and I'm speaking about, **now.**" He said, as he looked at both of them with a stern face. **"I mean it, yah hear. Get up, and get movin,"**

Jake looked at Tommy, sitting across the table from where he sat, a slight grin on his face that was saying, *Well, you lucky dog, you got another chance. Don't blow it!*

Tommy and Molly got up at the same time. Molly knew better than to cross her father, anyway, as bad as she felt she was hoping that Tommy would finally understand; she wasn't a kid anymore. Tommy was so glad to have a chance to talk to her before he left, that it was hard for him to control his excitement. But he had to keep it in check, he wasn't about to let her turn the table on him. *He had to be strong,* he thought, *after all he was a man.* None the less, it was hard to control how he was really feeling.

As they headed for the door, Mr. McGregor said in a firm voice, "I want the two of you to leave here holdin hands and I want you to return the same way." He waited to see what they would do. When they just looked at each other, McGregor yelled, **"I mean now, damn it, and don't come back until holdin**

hands is what you want to do." The shock of what he said caused them both to jump, and then look at each other, as they quickly took each other's hand and walk out the door.

The touch of Molly's hand in Tommy's caused him to tremble a little, and his heart picked up its pace. He wasn't expecting that kind of a feeling, but it was really nice. *Wow,* he thought, *I can't believe I feel this good from just touching her hand. My heart is beating a mile a minute; I wonder if this is what she meant about a woman's feelings? Do women have feelings like this too?*

Molly too, was excited. The fourteen year old girl had never touch a boy in an intimate way. The touch of Tommy's hand in hers caused all kinds of feelings to start running through her body: she felt like she was shivering, but she wasn't cold; her heart started to beat faster and she started breathing heavier. And that quivering that she felt in her stomach seemed to rest there. It was a real good feeling.

They started walking in the direction of the barn. Tommy made an attempt to break the ice. "Molly," he said, "I'm real sorry about what happened last night. I don't know exactly what happened or what I said that was wrong, but I'm real sorry that I hurt you, and that's a fact."

She said nothing for a few minutes as they continued to walk. She was feeling quite nervous about her feelings and what they meant. She heard Tommy's apology but she wasn't sure how to respond. If she let him off of the hook too easy he might make that mistake again. But on the other hand, she wanted desperately to forgive him. She knew that her pa was right, she never had eyes for anyone but Tommy and she didn't want him to leave without them at least being friends. "I'm not sure how to respond to that Tommy," She said. "I think you were thoughtless, and rude, and it did hurt me. After all, I am really a woman; maybe not quite full grown yet, but then, neither are you." She paused for a minute. He didn't respond. "I do forgive you Tommy, but will you start treating me more like a woman from now on? Will you listen to what I have to say, and try to understand me?"

Tommy turned to face her as they walked, "Sure, I'll treat you anyway you want, I just want us to be friends."

"Friends," she said, "that would be nice." But she knew in her heart that she wanted to be more than friends. She knew she was in love with him, but wondered if he would ever feel that way about her. *Well*, she thought. *Friends, for now, would be nice.*

"Yeah," he responded. Although his true feelings were a lot deeper, he said what he thought she wanted to hear. They both started to swing their hands as they walked toward the barn. He gently squeezed hers and she responded likewise. They slowly walked into the barn and Tommy motioned towards a bale of hay, and they sat down. She was holding his hand as they sat down and drew his hand into her lap.

He was instantly aware that his hand was resting on her upper thigh, and his hormones were paying attention. She may have been wearing a dress and petticoat but he could still sense her thigh there. He was closer to a girl... err woman than he had ever been. He was afraid she might realize where his hand was and throw it away. He hoped she wasn't aware. He was feeling so good that he didn't want this moment to end.

She wasn't thinking about his hand touching her thigh only about how nice it felt to hold his hand. His hand felt nice in her hand; and she could sense his nervousness because she was nervous too. As a matter of fact, it felt wonderful just to touch him anywhere. Holding hands, at that moment, was the most wonderful thing she could image doing.

But Tommy was beginning to get other ideas. He wanted to hold her, and maybe even kiss her. He turned to her and said, "Molly, you are without a doubt the prettiest girl I've ever seen."

Her heart fluttered as she looked him in the eye. She couldn't believe that he said that; if she was a stick of butter, she would have melted. "Thanks, Tommy, that's really sweet of you to say, and even nicer to hear." She never knew Tommy could say such sweet words. "Do you really think I'm pretty?"

"You bet you are, Molly" replied Tommy. "As I said before, you're the prettiest girl... err... I mean woman, I've ever seen." They both laughed together.

"I guess 'girl' is okay once in awhile," she said as they continued to laugh. She didn't want this moment to end. Tommy was saying things she never thought she'd hear him say, and she didn't want it to end.

He kept looking at her; she was even prettier when she laughed. His eyes dropped to her chest, and he watched as her chest rose and fell. He just had to get closer to her. He took his hand from hers and wrapped it around her back drawing her to him. She looked up into his eyes as his face moved closer to hers. *He's going to kiss me*, she thought. *Should I let him or push him away? Should, I turn my head to avoid his lips, or should I tell him no?* Suddenly it was too late his lips were on hers and they were electrifying, they were warm and soft and yes, sensual. She felt her breast rise and fall, and her breathing became erratic. What was happening? His lips felt warm as they moved over hers. Her skin felt tingly, and she became weak. She surrendered to the kiss.

He broke the kiss long enough to look into her eyes, "You certainly are a woman Molly, I love kissing you. Do you mind if I do it again?" His heart was beating so fast he was losing control; he had to have more.

"Oh Tommy," she said as she looked back into his eyes, "I feel so strange, I can't catch my breath, and I don't think we should kiss anymore."

But Tommy pressed on he had to kiss her again. She felt his lips once again on hers. The feeling was driving her crazy; she didn't know what to do. In all of her fourteen years she never experienced anything like this; it was driving her into wanton passion. She just didn't realize what was going on. In her young virgin state with no education about such matters she was putty in his hands. Lucky for her Tommy never realized it.

"Please Tommy," she begged, "you've got to stop. It just isn't right for us to be doing this." She pushed with all of her might against his chest and said, "Tommy, if you don't stop, I'm going to scream."

"But you're my woman Molly. I love you. I need you, and I don't know when I'll see you again. Please, don't tell me to stop."

He loves me, she thought. *I never thought I'd hear him say that. Oh Lord, what should I do?* She felt weak, but she knew she had to get control of the situation. Tommy had to stop.

"I'm serious Tommy, we can't kiss like this. It isn't right. What would my Pa say? What would your Pa say, or what would God say?"

God, Tommy thought. The words of his father suddenly came ringing into his ears: *"Walk in the Spirit and you shall not fulfill the lust of the flesh."*

Walk in the Spirit, Tommy thought. He hadn't found the Spirit anywhere since his parents died; and "lust of the flesh" that's certainly what he was feeling. Man he was a long way from God now. He silently prayed: *God, I'm so confused but thank you that Molly had the strength to stop me.*

When he came to himself, he slowly laid his head on her head. "God, Molly, you're the most wonderful thing that's ever happened to me. Please forgive me, I just got carried away. You are so wonderful and your kisses are something, I never imagined. Promise me that you'll forgive me, and wait for me till I come back."

Her hand was caressing the back of his neck and head, "There's really nothing to forgive Tommy, I wanted you to kiss me as much as you did, but I was afraid of where we were going; and of course I'll wait for you Tommy, I always have!" She said.

"Thanks Molly," he said. "I really never thought of you as a woman before, but I guess you are. As a matter of fact, you're more of a woman than I am a man. I don't think I could have stopped."

"Let's not talk about that anymore; you're going to be leaving in a little while let's just enjoy this time together." She loved being in his arms even his head resting on hers felt wonderful. She was feeling more like a woman now than she ever had, but it was going to end. Tommy was going to leave. She took a deep breath and asked, "Tommy, are you sure you really want to go?"

"It isn't something I have to think about," Tommy said, "I don't have any choice. I gotta get the men who killed my ma and pa. I won't rest until I do. Then I'll be back and we can be together."

"Oh Tommy, I wish you wouldn't go."

"I have to Molly. Will you pray for me while I'm gone?" *Pray for me,* he thought. *I guess, I really do need prayer. But I don't want to talk to God; he let me down when my family died.* He had forgotten already, he had just thanked God for giving Molly the strength to stop them.

"I'll pray for you day and night Tommy, but I really don't want you to go." Her heart was breaking but she knew she couldn't use stronger words to keep him. She knew he would leave.

"Please try to understand," he said. "I have to go."

"I'm trying to Tommy, but I don't know what to pray for; I don't think God wants you to kill anyone."

Tommy remembered that his father quoted a scripture that said something like *"The steps of a good man are ordered by the Lord'* and *'He would uphold him with His hand."* (Ps. 37:23-24) He wasn't sure if that would mean what it sounded like, but he liked the idea of letting God directing his path. Although it didn't seem like God was directing his father's path, he got killed. He was really confused where God was concerned.

"Molly," he said, "why don't you just pray that God will direct my path and keep me safe. If it is not God's will for me to kill those men, God will work it out. Is that okay?" He knew he was stepping out on a limb, because he was saying this for her comfort. He knew in his heart he wanted to kill those men.

"Yes," she said. "But I'll be praying that God directs your path back to me." After she said that, they hugged and kissed once more; only this time it was gentle kisses full of tenderness they both felt. He loved holding her next to him. She felt so warm and comforting. *It was definitely going to be hard to leave her now,* he thought. But he felt a compelling urge to avenge his parents. The men who killed them must not go unpunished. They held each other a few more minutes and then headed back to the house.

Jake told the McGregor's they were going to try and join a cattle drive that was headed down near Mexico. After they said their goodbyes they mounted up their horses and were on their way. Molly stood waving goodbye to Tommy with tears in her eyes. Tommy looked back over his shoulder as he rode away; *I'll be back*, he thought to himself as he waved to her. *I'll be back.*

As Molly looked at him riding off, her mind went back to earlier that day; she remembered those wonderful feelings that she shared with him. She was going to miss him terribly. She had always thought about them being together. Now, it was possible but only if he returned. *Oh God*, she prayed, *please keep him and Jake safe, and help them to do the right thing. Somehow Lord, bring Tommy back to me, and let your will be done in our life.*

She realized that she was in love with Tommy and hoped that he wouldn't be gone too long.

Chapter 6

J ake and Tommy rode for almost two full days before they reached the Handlebar Ranch. Each night along the way, they found time for target practice. Tommy was really impressed with the knowledge that his uncle Jake had. He was getting better all the time; but he had a long way to go if he wanted to be as good with a gun as his uncle. For now though, he was concentrating on being accurate. His uncle Jake told him that after he became accurate and could hit the target every time; he would be ready for the real lessons. He wondered what his Uncle meant by that, but he never asked.

As they rode up to the main house on the Handlebar Ranch, they noticed about twenty men milling around by the barn and the corals. Two men were standing on the porch watching them approach.

"You Mr. Crawford," Jake said.

"Yeah, I'm Crawford." One of the men said.

"I'm Jake Wade. I heard you were looking for some cowboys to help drive a herd south."

"You heard right. You say your name is Jake Wade?"

"Yeah, and this is my nephew Tommy."

"Jake Wade! I think I've heard of you. Are you a bounty hunter?"

"Maybe," Jake said. He knew the question would be asked.

"Are you as good with a gun as they say?" asked Crawford.

"Probably," Jake knew they would be looking for protection along the way, and thought he needed to give them a more direct answer to this question.

Crawford stared at him a moment as he thought, *If this is the Jake Wade that I have heard about, he is fast with a gun, but he is also good with cattle.* "You ain't in any trouble are you?"

"None that I can't handle; but there's no posse looking for me if that's what you mean."

Mr. Crawford thought for a few more minutes as he looked Jake over then said, "I also heard you were pretty good with cattle."

"I can get a herd where it's goin, if that's what you mean."

"Good," said Crawford. "What I'm really looking for is a trail boss to lead the herd. All of these men that you see here are good cattle men; they know what to do with a herd. What I need is someone tough who knows the trail, and can lead these men to where their goin. From what I hear, you could be the man. However, I don't know about little Tommy there."

"Tommy's with me. I told you he was my nephew his ma and pa were killed by a varmint a few months ago. We need to go after the men who did it; we hear they may have gone to Mexico. Tommy needs to stay with me. He'll learn to be a good cattle puncher to, and you'll be glad he came. We stay together, or we leave together, your choice."

"Wait a minute," said the man who was standing next to Mr. Crawford, "you say you're Jake Wade? I understand he's pretty good with a gun. Are you that Jake Wade or not?"

"I don't know how many Jake Wade's there are mister, I only know I'm Jake Wade. Who are you?"

"I'm Buster Lloyd, I'm the foreman here, and I look after Mr. Crawford's interests. Now, are you that Jake Wade, the one that is good with a gun, or not?"

Jake stood there looking at Buster for a few minutes sizing him up, "I may be him, why?"

"Cause, I'm pretty good with a gun myself. Maybe I want to see how good you are."

Jake got a real mean look in his eyes that Tommy had not seen before, and said to Buster, "Are you talkin about a shoot out, do you want to draw against me?"

Buster was caught a little off guard because that wasn't exactly what he had in mind. "No! No! I don't want to draw against you" he said, getting a little nervous. "I'm no gunfighter. I don't want to see nobody get killed. I just thought we could shoot at a target or something."

Jake stood there a minute longer and thought over the situation. He looked around him and the other cowboys were beginning to gather in order to see what was going on. Jake thought that if he wanted to be the trail boss, it might be good to give them a little demonstration. Maybe a show of bullets would be something they would understand. He looked around him again for a target. The coral was about fifty yards away and the top rail of that fence would be sufficient, and no one was between him and the fence. He turned and looked at Crawford then turned as quickly as a rattle snake uncurling to strike; while turning he drew his gun and fired six shots as quickly as he could fanning the hammer of the gun. Each bullet found its mark in the top rail of that fence. He spun his gun twice and slipped it back into his holster. He turned to Buster and said, "You're turn!"

Buster stood there looking at the rail as his face got red with embarrassment. Then he turned and looked around at the faces of the men standing there. "I ain't ever seen anyone draw and shoot that fast and every one of them bullets hit the target. I recon you are Jake Wade."

Tommy spoke up then, "And I'll tell you all, he can do the same thing with the rifle. I seen him do it."

Jake pulled his gun from its holster and slowly began to reload it as he glanced around at the faces of the men who had gathered.

"Is that enough for you Buster?" said Crawford. "What do you men think? Do you think he would make a good trail boss? Could you all follow him?" As Crawford looked around the crew each one was shaking his head yes. "Good enough. Looks like you... and Tommy got a job. Only one thing, you have to give me your word you're gonna stay with the herd until it's delivered. I don't want you going after your prey till my cattle get taken care of."

"I can give you my word on that," said Jake.

"Tell me," asked Crawford, "Who are these men you're goin after."

"We don't know their names. All we know is there were four of them, they were Mexican's, and one of them that did the shootin, was all dressed in black."

"Damn," said Crawford, "I think your talkin about Eduardo and his gang. A bunch of bad hombres wanted for all sorts of things. You could get a bounty on them boys if you get em. Problem is they'd shoot you in the back first. You'd better keep your eyes open if you're goin after them."

"It isn't anything you need to be concerned about," said Jake. "As long as those boys don't come after your herd we won't meet them till near Mexico, and Tommy and I will take care of that. If they do come after your herd it will just happen sooner than we expect, that's all."

Tommy stuck his chest out. He was so proud to be riding with his uncle Jake that he couldn't speak. He was amazed that he could hit the rail on that fence that far away. If he could learn to be as good with a gun as his uncle Jake, no one could bother him.

Mr. Crawford looked at Jake and Tommy and said, "You boys can bed down in the bunk house with the rest of the hands tonight. Tomorrow after breakfast, we'll be round up the herd and be ready to make the trip to the stockyard outside Dallas. I plan on leavin two hundred cattle here. Buster, Hank, Jimmy and Fussy there," he pointed to the men, "will stay here and take care of them. The rest of us will be movin about three thousand head down to Dallas, Texas. Have you ever been to Dallas before Jake?"

"No... but I hear it's the city to see in Texas."

"You're darn tootin it is," said Buster, "I sure wish I could be a goin, but somebody's gotta stay here and take care of the ranch. I guess that's me," he said as he looked at Mr. Crawford.

"Sorry," said Mr. Crawford, "Maybe next time Buster. You know you're my right hand man here and somebody's gotta stay."

"Yea, I know boss," said Buster.

At that time, the cook walked out on the other end of the porch and began to ring a bell. He looked around at the men gathered, especially Jake and Tommy, but he said nothing as he turned and walked back inside.

Buster clapped his hands together and said, "Well there goes the dinner bell, reckon it's time to chow down."

They all started to head toward the mess hall and the beef stew special.

Jake and Tommy got to work with the rest of the crew the next day as they rounded up the herd and separated them from the ones that were staying. It took a few more days to get everything ready.

As Crawford had said, he left about two hundred head of cattle with the four men who stayed behind; the rest of the cattle would be driven to the Dallas stockyard.

Three thousand head of cattle is a lot for eighteen men, but Mr. Crawford said they might pick up a few more men along the way. Jake was hopeful, it would make the journey a lot easier. One can never tell if there are rustlers around or not; you just had to stay alert that meant keeping the guards awake at night. The more men they had, the easier that would be.

Everything seemed to be going smoothly as they moved the herd south. Jake told Tommy they wouldn't be getting a lot of target practice in because he didn't want to spook the herd. But Tommy could continue to practice drawing and aiming. Jake showed him how to oil his holster so he could get his gun our faster. He was teaching him how to lean to one side from the waist to avoid a direct hit. They practiced drawing and rolling on the ground; some of the hands that were around practiced some too.

Jake was pleased that Tommy was getting good at getting his gun out fast and pointing it from the hip, however, teaching him to aim and fire from that position was going to take some time; time he was afraid that they wouldn't have.

Meanwhile, down Mexico way, Eduardo and his men crossed the Rio Grande. They were leaving Mexico headed toward Del Reo, and up to Comstock Texas. Eduardo knew the taking was good, and the law enforcement in these two towns was poor. That meant easy takings for the likes of him and his men. They had rested in the little town of Nueva Rosita, Mexico for the past six months until their money ran out. Nueva Rosita was a quaint little town of a few hundred people it was big enough for fun and excitement and yet not big enough to draw attention.

It was now time to head back up toward Oklahoma. The circle in the past had proved profitable and entertaining for all of them. Now it was time to hit the circle again. The plan was to hit the smaller towns in West Texas on the way to Oklahoma and then return through East Texas.

Ah Oklahoma, Eduardo was reminiscing. Oklahoma was a fertile territory for him and his men. He remembered it well. The women there were quite entertaining, but he was saddened when he remembered the one that he had shot so fast. She was a lovely lady, and he would have really enjoyed her company. What was the name of that town... oh yes, it was Chickasha. The name he remembered had something to do with the Indian's that lived in that area. But that lady, wow! She was indeed a looker. If she just hadn't of run up on him that fast she might still be alive. He remembered firing without even thinking. Usually he never thought about anyone he killed, but she was an exception. Truth be told, he never really wanted to kill anybody, all he wanted was what they had.

Eduardo found out that it was more profitable for him and his men, if they robed the farmers and small ranchers, more so, than holding up banks. There was less chance of them getting caught or killed, and the women were very entertaining. There wasn't anything like an unwilling woman. He loved to hear them plead and beg not to be touched; but in the end he knew they really enjoyed being roughed up. One thing was for sure, if he let them live they would never forget the encounter. That was one of the reasons he rarely killed women he made love to, he wanted them to remember him. But, if they hurt him, or angered him, he wasn't against killing them. For that matter, he wasn't against killing anyone for any reason. He just wanted to leave them alive so he could come back later and help himself to what they had. Dead people don't produce anything.

He had picked up four more men in Nueva Rosita. When they hit the first farm outside Del Reo, Texas, he would find out what they were made of. If they didn't work out he would kill them. As far as he was concerned, hombre's who rode with him either lived to do what he said, or they didn't live. This is how he kept them in check; they knew he was cold and calloused, ruthless and yet trustworthy, a man of his word. Plus, he was dangerous with a gun or a knife, fast, tricky, sharp and accurate. He was the man to be with if you were a thief and a killer. He would lead the way, and yet, stay beside you backing you up with his life. Eduardo was a fierce leader!

The next day as they neared the town of Del Reo, they came upon their first farm, all eight men road up to the farmhouse. The farmer Dan Maxwell was working in the field when he saw them riding up. *This doesn't look good*, he thought. He immediately pulled his rifle from its holster on the plow, and headed for the house.

Eduardo had dismounted and was knocking on the door. Mrs. Maxwell had seen them riding up and was waiting for her husband to come. She stood inside the door shaking and very nervous. Her children were outside tending to the livestock and there wasn't time to say or do anything, she was just praying for their safety.

"Hey," Eduardo said, as he turned and motioned with his head for his men to look for others. "Is anybody home?"

Mrs. Maxwell said nothing.

Eduardo banged on the door again. "Come on Señora we know you're in there. We're just passin through and hope to get a little food, and then we'll be on our way."

Mrs. Maxwell knew she had to do something. Maybe if she was nice to them they would leave peacefully and no one would get hurt. She slowly opened the door and peaked out, "I was in the back room folding clothes. Can I help you gentlemen?"

"Si Señora," Eduardo said. "We've been on the trail for a few days and we need to get some food. We wonder if you could spare us a meal."

She was afraid of these men and didn't know how to react. She certainly didn't want to invite them in. As she looked out into the field she could see her husband coming to the house.

"We don't have much Señor, and you have quite a few men to feed, but I guess we can share what we have," said Mrs. Maxwell.

"That's all we ask," said Eduardo, "is to share with us what you have." He could see her now. She was a weather beaten woman of about thirty; farm life had been ruff on her, but she wasn't bad looking. She probably had a few kids around someplace, and they could see her old man working in the field when they rode up. He was a farmer and wouldn't present a problem sharing what he had. If he didn't want to, he wouldn't live.

Eduardo thinking as he looked at the woman, *he would be the first one to take her then the other men could have her. One of the reasons for raping the women, other than the pure pleasure it brought, was the fear factor. They would be too ashamed to tell anyone what had happened to their family; they would fear what others would think of them. So the whole family would live with the secret, and he could go on doing what he loved to do.*

"Can I help you?" a voice said behind him. It was Mr. Maxwell.

"Si Señor," said Eduardo. "I was just asking your Señora here, if she could spare a meal for me and my hombres."

Mr. Maxwell stood there holding his rifle in front of him at his waist, *what should he do*, he thought. He knew these men could be dangerous, and he had heard about a band of Mexican's that were looting farms; and there were too many of them to handle all alone. *Maybe*, he thought. *If I gave them some food and treated them well, they would leave in peace.*

"Sure," said Mr. Maxwell. "I think we can spare some vitals with you all." He lowered the gun down to his hips, "a man can't be too careful around his home these days. You all can clean up over there by the well til ma gets the food ready."

"Si, Señor," said Eduardo. He was never afraid of a man standing in front of him holding a gun. "I'm sure glad you lowered that gun."

Mr. Maxwell could tell by the way he said that sentence that if he had not lowered the gun he would be dead. He now began a silent prayer that God would protect his family from these men who could do him and them great bodily harm. He walked to the door to tell his wife Ruth to start supper. The man who was standing in the doorway and who had done all of the talking suddenly grabbed a hold of his rifle. "I think we should hold on to this for a little while, don't you," said Eduardo. Mr. Maxwell tensed up holding on to his rifle; he looked around at the other men who were standing there with their hands on their pistols and he knew he had no choice; he released his grip and

Eduardo took his rifle. *That was easy,* thought Eduardo, *now I know he won't cause any trouble; he just surrendered.*

"Hey Eduardo, look what we found," said one of his men. He was bringing up a boy and girl. It was the Maxwell's two children, Jenny was sixteen and Billy was twelve. Eduardo couldn't tell their ages, they looked like teens, he wasn't sure, and he didn't care. He kept eyeing little Jenny. Now she was a sassy Señorita. *Yes,* he thought to himself. *I thought her mother would be my first, but now, I have a better choice. 'Ah' the delights of life,* he thought.

"Bring them into the house," said Eduardo. "And you four hombres," he said as he pointed out four men, "You stay outside and make sure we're not disturbed till I tell you to come in, Si." They all nodded.

Mr. Maxwell didn't like the sound or that statement. He was afraid of what he meant about 'not being disturbed.'

Eduardo stood in the doorway as the children passed by him; he was especially interested in Jenny. She was very pretty, a delicate morsel for these parts. Today, she would learn about survival and also about love. He was sure he could control the father; the mother he wasn't concerned about.

Mrs. Maxwell had Jenny set the table while the men stood around and watched. Jenny's father sat at the table where he was told. She didn't like the idea of these men telling her father what to do. It wasn't like him to listen to others and yet he was doing what he was told. He must be afraid of something that happened before her and Billy got here. She didn't know what it was but it made her feel very uncomfortable. These men were all Mexicans. What were they doing on this side of the boarder? After she finished setting the table, she went over and stood by her mother, who was stirring the stew.

For the next forty-five minutes no one said anything. They just stood there looking at each other. Jenny was feeling more and more uncomfortable, especially because Eduardo kept his eyes on her. She knew he was looking her up and down. She wondered what his intentions were but she was afraid to think about it.

"Suppers ready," said her mother, "you can all find yourself a place around the table, and Jenny and I will serve you."

Eduardo sat at the head of the table and said, "Señora, I think you can serve everyone, and your daughter can sit next to me, 'a place of honor' so to speak, Si."

Jenny looked at her mother; she didn't want to sit by that nasty man. Her mother looked at her father who just stared at her then she looked at Eduardo, "maybe she should sit by her father," she said.

"No, I think she should sit by me," he said as he leaned over and patted the chair on his right.

Her mother looked again at her father, who remained motionless, and then at her and nodded. Jenny obeyed and sat next to the man. He looked at her and smiled showing his crooked teeth. No sooner did she sit down than he reached out and touched her shoulder, patting it he said, "Relax Señorita, everything will be okay, Sí." She knew it would not be okay. She wished they were gone, but she nodded her head and kept her eyes looking downward.

No one said anything during the meal; they just looked from one to the other. Jenny felt that all of these evil men were looking at her. *If she could get a gun,* she thought. *She could make them all leave. Why wasn't her father ordering them to leave? Why was he so submissive? And why was her mother not saying anything.* She wasn't that much of a child that she didn't understand what was going on, but why not stand up to these men. However, she also knew the answer. They all had guns and she knew they would use them. She didn't know what to do, so she just played along. Then she realized what her parents were doing. They were playing along, perhaps buying time. She hoped this would be over soon and these terrible men would be gone. She prayed silently that God would send someone to help them.

When supper was over and the four men outside had traded places with the three inside Eduardo said to Mr. Maxwell, "Señor, I wonder if you could help us out. We are running low on supplies, and need some help in order to move on."

Jenny's father said, "We don't have much money, all of it is tied up in feed and stock. We won't have anything til harvest." *My God,* he thought. *I hope they don't take everything we've got.*

"Well, then tell me Señor, how much livestock do you have that you can share?"

"I can't share anything," said her father. "If I gave you anything, then we would have to struggle to survive."

"Ah, the magic word my friend," said Eduardo. "You see that's what we are doing now; we are surviving. So perhaps you could help us and we could help you, Si."

Mr. Maxwell was struggling now. He knew they were going to be robbed, but if he gave them something maybe they would leave his family alone. He certainly didn't like the way Eduardo was treating his daughter. "Well," he said, "maybe we could spare something."

"Good Señor, I knew you would help us out. Why don't you and these two hombres" he said as he pointed to two of his men, "go and check on the livestock and see what you have."

Mr. Maxwell suddenly remembered he had left the mule hooked to the plow, he hoped it was still there. He looked at his wife and children; he didn't want to leave them alone with these men, but he knew he had no choice. He looked at his wife and said, "I have to unhook the mule in the field." He said that to let his family know he would be gone for a while, they would have to fend for themselves. They nodded their heads that they understood.

Eduardo saw the exchange and smiled. "Why don't you take the boy with you, to help out," he said.

One of his men, Diego, quickly replied, "Hey Eduardo, maybe the boy should stay and help clean up in here."

Eduardo took that to mean that he wanted to have some fun with the boy. If that was his thing it was all right with him. "Pues Si," he said as he nodded at his man. "Señor, you can go with these two men now, and I want to know what you have that you can spare." He said this as he looked intently into the eyes of Mr. Maxwell. "Manuel, as you escort the Señor to the field tell Emilio and Santeago to come in here." He looked around the room at the rest of his men and said, "Except for Diego, the rest of you outside."

The father stood up and slowly walked out with the men, *God*, he prayed, *please protect my family.* When there was nothing else he could do, all he could do was trust.

He had no sooner left than Eduardo said, "I think we should have ourselves a fiesta. Diego, why don't you get your guitar?"

Diego smiled and said, "Pues Si, Señor!" He ran outside and got his guitar off his horse and was back in a few minutes. He started to play some Spanish song immediately upon his return.

Eduardo grabbed the hand of Jenny, and pulled her to her feet, "Come on Señorita, and let us dance." He quickly pulled her to him and started to twirl her around before she could reply. One of the other men grabbed her mother and began to dance with her. The other man went over and grabbed Billy, pulling him to his feet. Billy's mouth fell open as he looked in disbelief at the man, and then at his mother. The man began to dance with him.

Eduardo was dancing with Jenny and slowly pushed her backward until he reached the bedroom door. He quickly opened it and pushed her inside. "Ma," she yelled as he shut the door. Her mother could not reply, the man she was dancing with was kissing her as she tried to fight him off.

Eduardo stood there looking at Jenny, "Señorita, I want to see what you look like naked. Would you undress for me, or would you like me to undress you?"

"Please Señor; don't do this I'm a virgin. Please have mercy!" Her plea went unanswered as he began to rip her clothes from her body.

This is what Eduardo and his men did to every farmer and rancher throughout Texas, and Oklahoma. Everyone that lay in their path was robbed, raped or killed if necessary. No one was exempt. Jenny, her mother and brother were raped but no one was killed. Her father had given them whatever they wanted and the family survived. They left him with a cow, a bull and his chickens. They never completely stripped a family, because they might come this way again; who knows when they might need a little fun and supplies. *Anyway,* he thought, *he wasn't a completely evil man.*

If they came this way again the family would know what to expect. They were always left in fear for their lives. Those who were raped would have to deal with what had happened to them. They couldn't tell without embarrassing the family. For the most part, they kept their mouth shut. If they did tell the local authorities it was usually about them being robbed. But the authorities could read between the lines; why would a person give up their possessions without a fight, and evil men do evil things to women under their power. It could only be because they were protecting each other. Eduardo and his men would move the livestock to the closest town, and sell them. This they would continue to do until someone stop them.

Chapter 7

J ake had moved the herd across the border into Texas and was headed towards Dallas. Up ahead they saw an army patrol approaching them. Jake and Mr. Crawford rode out to meet them. It was the man leading the patrol that spoke first.

"Hello gentlemen," he said. "I'm Captain Frost of the United States Cavalry. Can I ask who's in charge of this herd?"

"I am," said Mr. Crawford, "there my cattle."

"How many head have you got there," asked the Captain.

"Three Thousand head," said Mr. Crawford. "We're on our way to Dallas. Is there a problem officer?"

"No sir, none indeed, we're just on a routine patrol. But now that you ask, we could use a couple a hundred head of cows at Ft. Worth; we have an army post there."

"I sure would like to oblige Captain," said Crawford, "but I don't have any men I can spare to split the herd."

"I understand," said the Captain. "But the army would spend good money to get them cattle delivered. What I was thinking is, when you get to Dallas you could cut out a couple a hundred from the others and take them to Ft. Worth."

"That's a good idea," said Crawford. "But how do I know that if I bring those cattle to Ft. Worth, someone there will buy them?"

"No problem there sir, I'll be returning to Ft. Worth in a few weeks and I'll let the quartermaster know about the herd. They'll send someone to Dallas to wait for you. Okay?"

"Sounds good," said Crawford. "Let me ask you Captain is there anything I should be aware of up ahead? You know like rustlers, or Indians."

"Well, you know you always have to be aware of cattle rustler's, that's one of the reasons we're on patrol. The Indians haven't been a problem in the past few years, except for Geronimo. He has been known to attack and rob in both Oklahoma and Texas, but that's rare because we believe he's from Arizona. However, there is a band of Mexicans we're looking for. I don't think they'll be a problem for you; they like to rob the farmers and ranchers. Personally I think they're a bunch of cowards that just pick on the weak, if you know what I mean."

"Yea," said Crawford. "But, I've known a lot of farmers and ranchers, and they can be a nasty bunch if you get em riled."

"That's the problem," said the Captain. "These men are doing something to their victims that scare them really bad. There almost afraid to talk about them. We do know they are Mexicans, and they are led by a man named Eduardo."

Jakes ears perked up. Crawford had mentioned this name before. "This man Eduardo, is he known to dress in black?"

"Yep; black everything, even his horse."

"Is he supposed to be in these parts?" Jake asked.

"Well, last we heard they hit a family down around Del Reo. We have a patrol headed that way too. The problem with this gang is that they seem to zigzag across the country and it's hard to catch them; at least that's why we think they haven't been caught so far. We're heading north then we'll work our way south and west. If you see them be on guard: there a bad bunch."

"How many is riding in his party," Jake asked.

"Last we heard he only had about seven or eight men. However, a man as ruthless as this Eduardo, could have a small army, the fact that he only has a few men, tells us a lot about him."

"What do you mean," asked Jake.

"Well, if he had a bigger band of followers it would be harder for him to hide and easier for us to catch him. We believe he keeps it small so he can operate the way he wishes and still be able to hide. If he had a larger group of men it would be much harder to hide, and sooner or latter, he would run head on into the United States Cavalry. The only ones who have been able to give the Cavalry trouble were Quantrill's Raiders and they were mostly Confederate Soldiers. Also I should add, he likes robbing the farmers and ranchers, he takes their cattle and drives them to the nearest town and sells them. If he had more men it would be more costly. This way he can feed himself and his men and take whatever he wants. We've also had reports of some rapes and we believe there are many more, but people are afraid to talk about those personal things, if you know what I mean."

"Yea, I know what you mean," said Jake. "You've given us a lot of information and a lot to think about. We'll be on alert; if we see any Mexicans, I'll try and send word." Jake was thinking as he spoke, that if they see any Mexicans, especially one dressed in black, there wouldn't be much to talk about; but he was trying to be courteous with the soldiers.

They said there farewells and the Cavalry continued on their journey northward. Jake and Crawford rode back to the herd. Jake had a lot on his mind. He wanted to leave the herd and go looking for them and he knew if he told Tommy he would too. But he had given Crawford his word and he would keep it. They were only a few weeks from Dallas, and Crawford and his men could take the two hundred head to Ft. Worth. As soon as Crawford paid them he and Tommy would go looking for those renegade Mexicans, and this guy called Eduardo.

The next couple of weeks were almost uneventful, unless you counted the roundup of stray calf's and cows. They kept the herd heading south toward Dallas. During this time, Tommy was trying to sort out what had happened back at the farm that day. It had been almost a year since his parents died and his anger had subsided considerably. At least he was able to deal with it now. At first he was so filled with bitterness that he could only think of killing those men who had killed his parents. But he realized now, that he was also angry with his parents.

As he remembered looking down from the hill that day at the scene below, his father was sprawled out on the ground face down with his right arm extended holding on to his rifle. Why was his father so far from the house? He would have seen or heard the men coming. The usual response was to stay in the house since it offered the best protection. He would have talked to the men from the doorway. That was the lesson he had repeated to Tommy over and over many times. What caused him to go outside; and he was at least fifty yards from the house, which meant he was going to the men, or was going somewhere, and was caught outside. It didn't make sense. He was angry at this father for being so foolish.

He was also angry at his mother. In his mind he remembered her running at the man in black. He didn't know she was actually running to aid his father. *She should have realized*, he thought, *her life was in danger.* He couldn't realize how hurt and shocked his mother was, because the love of her life was lying there dying. It is normal for a person going through shock to act irrational.

And what about him, he thought, *she wasn't thinking about him. If she was, she wouldn't have tried to attack that mad man.* Now Tommy was alone; neither of them where thinking or concerned about him. At that particular moment he hated his parents for leaving him alone.

He was also angry at himself. *Fishing*, he thought. Was fishing so important to him that day that he snuck out and skipped doing his chores? He had a great time that morning and caught a good number of fish. He couldn't wait to get home and show his dad. He knew his father would get over his disappointment about his chores, when he saw the fish he had caught. The only one he could think about that morning was himself. He loved to fish so much that it outshined everything else.

Now, he realized, he had not thought once about fishing in all this time. Fishing didn't seem to be as important anymore. Yes, he was angry with himself. Had he stayed home that day he would have been in the barn doing his chores. His rifle might still have been in the house, but he too would have heard the men coming and would have run to the house. His father was an expert with the rifle, and at that time he was pretty good himself. He could have helped his father and the two of them could have defended their home. *I would have told him not to go outside. But, I wasn't there. I went fishing.* Yes, he was angry with himself, but he was also angry with God.

He was angry with God because God did not keep his word. He did not protect his mother and father. He allowed these evil men to kill his parents and how many others. Where was God when this was happening? For that matter where was God and who was He, that He could let murderers and thieves continue to exist. What kind of a God would allow this evil?

Yes, he was angry with God. His father had been the pastor of the church in Chickasha, Oklahoma for as long as he could remember. His father never got paid for being a pastor. He remembered his father had said, the apostle Paul worked as a tent maker to support his ministry; therefore, he would work as a farmer.

He knew his father and mother loved God. They prayed at every meal, and early in the morning he could hear his mother praying in their bedroom. His father always had time to talk about God, and would stay up long after he went to bed to read the Bible by candlelight. He remembered his father in the field as he was pushing the plow, his lips would be moving and he would look up and down as though carrying on a conversation: he knew he was either praying or practicing a sermon. His pa was always willing to help someone in need, and sacrifice what he had for the sake of others. His father had talked about trusting God and not relying on our own understanding; but this made no sense at all to Tommy. If anyone was a Christian it was his pa. Why would God let such a tragedy happen? Especially to a man who had done so much for so many others? How can you trust a God, who makes no sense at all? Tommy was angry with his father for trusting God, but he was angrier with God.

Hate is a terrible thing! Hate causes pain and anger from the one who hurts us; it drives a person to want revenge. Tommy was so full of hate and anger that all he could think about was revenge. He wanted to kill the men who had caused him pain, and his pain caused him to blame everyone. He blamed his father: he blamed his mother he blamed God, and even blamed himself. Hate is a terrible thing!

Back home Molly was busy making a new dress. Her mother had taught her to make aprons and bonnets, and now, was teaching her to make a dress. A dress was a big deal; there was a lot of work and detail to making a new dress. She had carefully cut out the pattern for the dress with sleeves and full skirt, and was now; working on the dress, but her mind was somewhere else. She was thinking about Tommy. Before he had left he had kissed her. It was a warm passionate kiss that she just couldn't forget. He asked her to wait for him, and she was. She missed him so much. He had been gone for months. As she glanced out the kitchen window she wondered what he was doing, and when he would return. She could still feel his lips on hers as she remembered that kiss and his arms around her. He was a young man but he was very strong, she could feel his strength as he pulled her against him. As she pondered her thoughts, she felt warm and comforted, and yet, lonely for him. *Come home Tommy*, she thought. *Come home, to me.*

The herd was only a few days outside of Dallas, so Mr. Crawford went on ahead. He needed to find the cattle buyer and where to deliver the three thousand head of cattle. As he rode into Dallas, he noticed the bank, the hotels, the saloons and the sheriff's office. It was a thriving city in 1885 but it was by no means a metropolis. The Santa Fe Railroad had connected it as far east as Chicago Illinois, and as far west as San Francisco, California. Dallas was becoming one of the places to be, if you wanted notoriety.

J. W. Ditty was the sheriff and a good one. But this was troublesome times. A sheriff only served one or two years; they either were killed in the line of duty, or resigned because of the stress. J. W. was elected the year before, and was determined to clean up the city and make Dallas, a place of pride. He, as well as many others in Dallas, had heard of the renegade Mexican band that was robbing the farmers and small ranchers; but, he was powerless to do anything much about them. The Mexican band stayed mostly on the western side of Texas and the people of Dallas didn't want to get involved with other communities.

They were content to let the Texas Rangers take care of them.

The Texas Rangers had been looking for the Mexican band as well, but they proved to be a tricky bunch of thieves. By the time they heard where they had been, they were gone, and even following in the direction they thought they headed, proved wrong. They weren't sure where they were hiding, or even if they went back to Mexico after each raid. They had heard that they had been in Oklahoma, but didn't know if it was true or not. But the Texas Rangers always get their man, and they would get these Mexican thieves as well.

Mr. Crawford found the cattle buyer, and where the cattle would be kept. He also found the Army Quartermaster, who informed him that they could actually use three hundred head of cattle instead of the two hundred the Captain had said. They agreed on the three hundred provided the cattle buyer didn't have any objections, and Crawford and his men would take them to Ft. Worth. With all of his business finished he stopped by the Lazy Day Saloon for a quick drink, before leaving town. A cowboy had to clear the dust out of his mouth.

The saloon was a typical big city saloon with a stage in the front, where he supposed they had nightly entertainment; the piano player with a lady in colorful clothing would be singing nearby, and the menagerie of colorful people that filled the room. He supposed that was the town drunk that stood at the end of the bar slurping on his whiskey, and over in the corner was the poker table filled with players.

He ordered a double shot of whiskey and a beer from the bartender, and turned around to look the place over once again. He noticed a man approaching him from the right. The guy was a big man with a handlebar mustache. He was wearing a flannel shirt and jeans with a leather vest but they were worn from aging. He had a gun strapped to his side. "You new in these parts mister," the man said.

"Kind a, it's not the first time I've been to Dallas, but you might say I'm new," said Mr. Crawford.

"My names Curley, I run one of the livery stables here in town. I thought if you were going to be here for awhile, I might take care of your horse."

"Hi Curley, I'm John Crawford. I might take you up on that if I was going to stay for awhile, but I've got business outside of town."

"Well," said Curley, "you can't blame a guy for trying to drum up a little business."

"Not at all," said Crawford. "Can I buy you a drink?"

"Sure would appreciate it, and the next round is on me."

Crawford ordered Curley a drink then asked, "What kind of entertainment do they have here in the evening?"

"Those pretty girls over there," he pointed across the room, "they come out and dance, and they got a new singer that's about as good as I've ever heard."

"You don't say," said Crawford. "Maybe after I take care of my business my men and I might hang around town a few days."

"If you do, and you have a hankerin, you might bring your horses to my stable. It's Curley's Stable down the street. We'll take good care of them."

"We might have a deal Curley. But for now I'd best be headin out of town, I got a two day ride ahead of me I suppose."

After their drinks and goodbyes, Crawford mounted his horse and headed north to meet the herd.

Chapter 8

E duardo and his men were entering the town of San Angelo, Texas. It was the home of Ft. Concho, which housed the U.S. Cavalry, and the famous Black Cavalry, better known as the Buffalo Soldiers by the Indians. The town which lay along side of the Fort was a pretty thriving little town and was just recently named San Angelo. Eduardo thought he and his men could hold up there for a few days.

As they rode into town they noticed the people watching them. This was nothing new to them: they were Mexicans in an American city. They rode down the center of town to the local saloon. There they tied up their horses and dismounted. Eduardo looked around the town for any signs of trouble but all they saw were the curious crowds of spectators. *That was unusual*, thought Eduardo. *Why were they all standing around in small groups; some in front of the bank, some in front of the saloon across the street, and others standing outside the general store.* He looked up and down the street and saw only a few people crossing the street or walking on the sidewalks.

His men weren't paying any attention, they just headed inside the saloon as they laughed and joked with each other. Finally, Manuel noticed Eduardo looking up and down the street with a curious look on his face. He jabbed Emilio in the side and motioned toward Eduardo. Emilio turned and the others stopped and turned also. "What is it Eduardo," asked Manuel.

"Something is wrong Manuel. Look at all the people in this town... What do you see?"

Manuel and the others looked up and down the street and around the town. They turned and looked at each other nodding... something was wrong.

"Señor" said Manuel, "something smells bad, Si."

"Pues Si," said Eduardo. "Emilio, you and Manuel go across the street and ask the people in front of that saloon if something is wrong."

"Si Señor," said Emilio as he and Manuel started across the street.

The people across the street saw them coming and began to split up and go in different directions. Emilio and Manuel stopped in the middle of the street and turned around to look at Eduardo.

Eduardo was watching what had happened and turned again to look up and down the street. *What is going on*, thought Eduardo. *Maybe somebody recognized us and has set a trap. We need to vamoose.*

Eduardo looked at Emilio, and Manuel, and then turned to the others, and in a voice that they could hear said, "Vamoose." They all quickly walked to their horses and mounted up. Then taking another look around them, they slowly headed out of town. They kept watch on the windows and roofs as they went. There was no trouble leaving town but they were aware of the looks that people were giving them. They were not looks of curiosity or fear but looks of caution. Eduardo was sure that someone had recognized them.

As soon as they were out of town they burnt leather for about ten miles and then stopped to look behind them. After waiting about ten or twenty minutes they were sure that no one had followed them. Eduardo said, "Perhaps our years of traveling around Texas, and having fun, have come to an end, Si."

"Si!" said all of his men almost in unison.

"You think someone recognized us Eduardo," said Manuel.

"Si," said Eduardo.

"Shall we head for Big Spring or Abilene?" asked Emilio. "Or shall we go back to Mexico?"

"I think amigos," said Eduardo "we should find us a camp around here for the night and think over what we should do."

"Si," they all said.

They rode on until they found a quite valley by a stream. There they set up camp for the night. After they had unsaddled their horses, set up their bed rolls and started a campfire, they waited for Eduardo to speak.

"Amigos, I think we shall not be able to move any livestock anymore. The time has come to think of a new way of life. It was easy to take from the farmers and ranchers what we liked, but if we cannot sell our gifts, then they are useless. I think that we shall need to look for bigger stakes. Where can we get money and supplies in large amounts so that we can keep on the move?"

All of his men looked at each other and Emilio responded for all, "I think we have no choice but to help ourselves to a few banks. Perhaps if we hit them hard, and one after the other, we can high-tail it for home before they know where we are going."

"Ah, Emilio you are thinking almost correctly," said Eduardo. "We do need to get money and the banks have money, but whatever we do they know where we are going; we are Mexicans." Eduardo thought for a few minutes then said, "What we need to do is find a safe place to hold up on this side of the boarder. We can hit banks well away from our camp and return there safely."

"It sounds like a good plan Señor," said Emilio, "But where will we find such a place here in Texas?"

"Emilio, go to my saddlebags and bring me the map of Texas, and also of Oklahoma," said Eduardo.

"Si Señor," said Emilio as he headed for the saddle-bags that were next to their bunks. After retrieving the maps he returned to Eduardo. He and the others were sitting around the campfire. He handed the map to Eduardo.

Eduardo unrolled the maps and began to look at where they were and where they were headed. *What lay in this area*, he thought as he looked at the maps.

"We are just south of Abilene," said Eduardo, "If we pass Abilene about twenty miles to the west and go to this valley between Abilene and Wichita Falls we could set up camp there. From there we could hit the stagecoaches going into Abilene and Wichita Falls a few times. Then we could go for the big enchilada, the bank at Wichita Falls, and cross the border into Oklahoma. The Texas rangers won't cross the border so all we would need to watch out for was the Cavalry or a posse." Although he wasn't aware of it, the last statement was not true. The Texas Rangers held to no legal system as to where they went to get their man. Not that they would go to Oklahoma, but it they needed to they would. His men weren't aware of it either; if they were they might have made other plans, or maybe not.

"Si," said all of his men as they looked from one to the other and shook their heads yes.

"This is a good plan," said Manuel. "Stopping stagecoaches would be a lot easier than taking money from a bank. Banks are in cities, and in cities you have a lot of people. A stagecoach only has two people on top, easy targets."

Eduardo, for the first time that he could remember, considered the opinion of his men. He realized that he would need their help to survive. He looked at them and said, "is everyone in agreement?" He couldn't believe that he was asking for their vote. Before this time they either did what he wanted or else they didn't live. But this was a new day. From now on they would have to trust each other because they needed each other. As he looked at all of his men, they understood what was happening, and one by one they nodded their heads yes.

In Dallas, Crawford had sold his entire herd, except for the three hundred head he would take to Ft. Worth. But he had a problem; he had received word that his foreman Buster, was gravely ill and not expected to live. The message didn't say what the sickness was, but it was urgent for him to return, he needed to go back to his ranch. He had to persuade Jake to take the herd to Ft. Worth. Jake and the rest of his men were at the Lazy Day Saloon, so he headed there.

Tommy was standing next to Jake, at the bar, in the Lazy Day Saloon. He was watching the people in the room. He had just tried his first shot of whiskey and determined it was not for him. His father, the preacher, wasn't a drinker. It wasn't because he had anything against drinking, as a matter of fact; he thought social drinking, as he called it, was okay.

But for him, as a preacher, he felt he had to set an example of discipline, so he never drank. This may have been the reason that Tommy felt uncomfortable about drinking, but it wasn't the reason he decided not to drink: he didn't like the taste, and it burned his throat. *Why would anyone want to drink that stuff*, he thought.

As he looked around the room he saw a young woman standing by the piano. She seemed to be about his age, but she reminded him an awful lot of Molly. What in the world was she doing in a place like this? He couldn't imagine Molly here. *Surely, that young lady is for sale*, he thought. Then he scolded himself for thinking such a thing. *It may be true, but if she was that kind of girl*, he thought. *Who was he that he could judge her?* He didn't know why she was here, or what brought her to this place. Then he realized, he sounded a lot like his pa, the preacher.

His pa was always ready to help others, and was very critical of those who judged other people because of how they lived, or what they had to do to survive. *Survive*, he thought. *That's probably what that young woman is doing.* He felt a deep sadness in his stomach for the young woman, and that sadness changed to longing when he started to think of Molly.

Tommy began to think about the last few days he had spent with Molly. He hadn't thought too much about her on the drive because he was busy, but here looking at that young woman brought back those precious memories. He remembered kissing her and holding her and then he longed to kiss her again. He remembered the excitement he felt at just holding her hand; then he looked back at the young woman again and she was going upstairs with a cowboy. He turned to Jake and said, "I think I'll take a walk and see what's happening around this town, okay."

"Sure Tom," said Jake. "You be careful out there, and remember, we're not from around here."

The name 'Tom,' caught him by surprise. *That was the first time he called me by a grown up name*, Tommy thought. *Maybe he's finally beginning to see me as a man.* "Yea, I will," he said, as he nodded and headed for the door. He went outside and looked up and down the street. It was Saturday afternoon about 3:00. He could see other cowboys coming into town. *Not much happening*, he thought. Then he noticed a little white church at the end of town.

His father had been the pastor of a church something like that one. He started heading down the street toward the church, not really knowing why. The closer he got the more he thought about his ma and pa. Ma was a Sunday school teacher and had taught him all that he knew about the Bible. The Bible was a good book he was thinking, but he never really took it seriously.

He got to the door of the church and found it open. He went inside and sat down in a pew. Looking around the church, he counted twelve pews on each side and three up in front of the church. *That's where the choir sits*, he thought. Then he looked at the pulpit and imagined his father standing there with one hand on the pulpit and the other pointing at the congregation. His father was a good preacher; he remembered that he always liked to hear what he had to say. As he sat there thinking about his father, and the sermons that he preached, tears began to roll down his face. *Pa*, he thought, *I'll never hear another sermon from you again.* He began to sob uncontrollably as he realized his love for his mother and his father.

"Tommy!" Tommy looked up and then began to look around the church. There was no one there. He was sure he heard someone call his name. "Tommy!" There it was again, yet he could see no one. "Tommy!" the voice said. "I love you!"

"Who is it, whose there?" he said.

"Who can speak to you that you cannot see? Who can speak to you that you cannot hear with your ears? Who loves you more than your mother and father?"

No it can't be, said Tommy to himself. *I must be hearing things.*

"You're not hearing things Tommy, I love you!"

You can't love me, and if you think I'm going to believe in you now, you must be kidding yourself.

"But I do love you!"

If you really loved me, why did you let those awful men kill my parents? What kind of God are you anyway?

"I'm the God who loves you, as I loved your parents."

How could you love anyone and let them be killed?

There are many things you don't understand, but I will teach you by and by."

Teach me! I don't want you to teach me anything. I don't even want to talk to you. What do you want from me anyway?

"I want to use you to glorify my name."

Glorify your name! You can't be the God that I've heard about, if you were, then you would know, the last thing I am going to do, is glorify your name.

"But you will glorify my name."

You can't be the God that my father loved, and I don't want to hear from you again. Get away from me and leave me alone. I hate you and there is no way I could ever serve you, let alone glorify your name. Tommy jumped up holding his ears and ran out the door. He started up the street towards the saloon but the voice kept following him.

"Tommy!"

Tommy held his ears, he didn't want to hear from God; he didn't want to talk to Him.

"Tommmmy! The voice was fading.

"Get away from me, and leave me alone. I don't believe in you."

"Tommmmmmy."

"Tommmmmmmy."

Tommy uncovered his ears as he walked into the saloon he went to a table in the rear and sat down.

Nothing!

He didn't hear anything. The voice was gone.

Good riddance, he thought. *How could He ever think that I would, or even could, want to serve Him?*

He was only sitting there a few minutes when he heard a woman's voice say, "Hi cowboy, you lonely?"

He looked up at the young woman he had seen early, the one that reminded him of Molly. "What?" he said.

"I said, are you lonely?"

"Maybe, maybe not," he said.

"I'm Cindy."

"Hi Cindy, I'm Tom."

"Mind if I sit down," she said.

"No," he said. *She really was a pretty one.* He thought.

"I saw you lookin at me earlier, but you didn't say anything."

"I got a lot on my mind. I'm afraid, I won't be good company tonight," he said.

"Well," she said, "I don't mind sittin here talkin for a bit if you buy me a drink. It's part of the policy of this establishment."

Establishment, he thought. *That was quite a word for a saloon girl. Oh, there I go again.* "Sure, I don't mind buying you a drink."

"What are you havin?"

He didn't want anything to drink and certainly not whiskey, but he thought he had to drink something, so he said, "I'll just have glass of beer," he said.

She left him sitting at the table as she went to the bar to get the drinks. He looked over at the bar and saw Jake looking at him. He nodded at Jake, and Jake, nodded back. She came back with the drinks and sat down.

"You know," she said, "we might get better acquainted if we went upstairs to a room."

"I don't think that would be a good idea."

"You're not a virgin are you?" she asked.

"No!" he lied. "Why would you ask that?"

"Well, you're kind a young and you could be."

"Well I'm not," he lied again.

"Why don't we go upstairs where we can talk," she asked again.

"As I said before, I don't think that's a good idea."

"Why not, you're not afraid of women are you?"

"No," he said as his mind went to Molly. He wondered what she would say if she could see him here with this woman. He also began to wonder what his intentions were with this woman. "I'm not afraid of anyone. I gotta girl back home and I want to be true to her."

"Where are you from cowboy?"

"Chickasha."

"Chickasha, I never heard of Chickasha," she said.

"It's in Oklahoma."

"Oh," she said. "Oklahoma is a long way away from here. How will she know what you are doing here? I think your secret will be safe with me."

Tommy was still angry with God about the conversation they just had. *Glorify His name indeed*, he thought. *It would serve Him right if I went upstairs with this woman. I could sleep with her that would show Him I don't want to serve him at all, but what about Molly?*

"She may not know," he said, "but God will know; He knows everything." *Where in the world did that come from?* He was shocked and angry with himself for bringing God into this. He didn't want God in this conversation. He didn't want God, anywhere.

"Wow," she said. "You sure know how to kill a mood. What are you some religious dude?"

"No, I just mean some things can't be hidden. I mean, my girl may not know from you or from me, but she knows God."

"You mean God is going to tell her?"

"Do you think it is impossible for God to speak to people?" He was wondering what he was saying and yet it seemed so natural.

"I don't know if God ever speaks to anybody; he never spoke to me, so how would I know? Has He ever spoken to you?"

She had him now; he wasn't sure how to answer that question. Just a few minutes ago he was telling God how much he hated Him, now he was talking about Him. *What's going on,* he thought. *The woman clearly needs help and I want to help her, but I don't know how, and I certainly don't want to talk about God.* He began to remember his father's sermons on how God talks to you.

"God," he said, "speaks to us in many different ways, doesn't He? I mean, from the beginning of time men have heard God speak in one way or another."

"Like how?" she said.

Tommy couldn't believe he was saying these things. He didn't want to talk about God but he couldn't seem to stop himself. "Well, I believe God speaks to us in at least three different ways. That is, if we are listening. He speaks to us primarily though his Word the Bible: we read it and He speaks through it. Then He speaks to us through other people, like me talking to you right now. And then, He speaks to us in a way that we can hear and yet there is no sound. It's like being connected to him in a spiritual way. Does that make any sense?"

"I'll tell you what cowboy; He never spoke to me in any of those ways so I don't know."

"He's speaking to you right now, through me." His mind went back to the church where God said to him that he wanted to use him to glorify Him. Suddenly he felt something that he had not felt in years. It was that feeling he had at church when the choir was singing and his father asked people to give their hearts to the Lord. He remembered going up front, and praying that night, and how he felt. It was the same feeling that he was feeling now. *Was God giving him these words to speak?*

She stared at him for a few minutes and said, "If God is speaking to me through you, then what does God want me to know?"

He looked at her and suddenly felt an over abundance of love flowing into him from the outside. *This must be how God feels towards this woman, if so, God must really love her.* "God wants me to tell you that he loves you, and He knows what you are going through. He wants to help you, if you will only trust him."

"You say, he knows what I am going through, and he wants me to trust him."

"That's what He just told me. He wants you to trust Him."

All at once, her heart was broken. Tears began to fill her eyes and flow down her cheeks and she began to sob quietly. *How could he possibly know what I am going through: from losing my parents and the farm I had grown up on, to being forced to moving into town, to entering this life of prostitution, to not having any way out, and longing somehow that God would help me?* "How do you know what I am going through? You don't even know me?" She said.

"I told you, I might not know, but God knows everything."

"If he knows everything then why doesn't he help me get out of here? I'm trapped. I don't have anywhere to go."

Good Lord, he thought. *Now I've put my foot in my mouth. How can I help this woman?*

"Can you ride a horse" he said. *Where did that come from?* He thought.

"What do you mean? I can't just leave. A girl like me has made too many mistakes to turn their life around. No one wants a woman like me unless they pay for her."

"If you continue to trust in yourself then you will die young and alone in this place. If you trust in God, He will turn your life around." He couldn't believe the words that were coming out of his mouth. Was he prophesying to this woman her fate?

She had her head bowed down and her tears were falling on the table, "If I had a horse, and I got on a horse, where would I go?"

Good question, he thought. *Now what am I going to do?* "You can come with me." *What! I'm on a cattle drive, how can she come with me?*

"Come with you, but you said you had a girl."

"I don't mean like that. I mean like a friend. I want to be your friend. Will you let me be your friend?"

"You mean, get on a horse and follow you back to Oklahoma?"

"You can do that if you want to; we got a beautiful farm back there. But you can stop anywhere along the way that you want to, no strings attached. I'll help you go anywhere that I can. What do you say?"

She sat there clearly stunned and thought, *this man is young but he knows about me and is willing to help me. How does he know? Could it be that God sent him to help me?* It was her way out, and she had to take it. After all, she had asked God for help. "Okay," she said. "But I don't have a horse, and I don't have any riding clothes."

"No problem. I can get you a horse and saddle and you can probably ware some of my clothes." *Why am I doing this?* He thought. *It's a good thing I just got paid.* But then he realized he was doing this because he really wanted to help this woman. He felt so good inside because he was listening to her, and now offering to help her. *Was this God?* He questioned.

"Where are you staying?" he asked.

"I have a room in back with the rest of the girls."

"Can you leave in the morning with no problem?"

"Yes!" she said. But what about tonight if I'm going to change my life it must be now." She realized that she could not take another night with some guy she never knew. It had to be now or never.

This caught him by surprise. What could he do? Then he had an idea, he was getting a lot of them recently. "What if I rented a room for you tonight as though you were staying with me?"

I would love to spend the night with this young man: I could show him things he never thought of. She was thinking. Then she caught herself, *what am I thinking, here is a man that honestly wants to help me and I've got my mind in the gutter.* "I'm sorry," she said. "Yes I think that would work."

He was confused, *what was she apologizing for?* It didn't matter. "Okay," he said. "I'll make the arrangements.

"Thank you," she said. "I don't know how I can repay you." He was her knight in shining armor. Actually, God was her knight in shining armor, but God was using Tommy even if he didn't want to be used. God had to be smiling about this.

Tommy made the arrangements with the clerk and walked her to her room. "Stay here, and I'll meet you in front of the saloon early in the morning, okay?" He said.

"Yes," she said, "and thanks again." She kissed him on the cheek and he left.

As he was walking down the steps from her room, he saw Mr. Crawford come in through the swinging doors. Tommy noticed the worried look on his face and hurried down the stairs to see what was wrong. He spotted Jake and the others at the bar and quickly made his way toward them.

"Jake," said Mr. Crawford, "I've got a real problem." He paused and waited for a reply.

"What's wrong," said Jake.

"I just received word that my foreman Buster has taken sick and they don't know if he will live. The boy's been with me all his life: he's like my son. I need to go back to my ranch now and I've made an agreement to deliver these cattle to Ft. Worth. Can you do this for me?"

Jake stood there thinking about what Crawford said. He remembered Buster, he surely wasn't a boy, but he guessed he would be to Crawford. He glanced at Tommy, and was sure Tommy would go along with whatever he decided. "Well," he replied. "Tommy and I have business, but I suppose it wouldn't be that much out of the way. If you need me, I'll do it."

"Thanks," said Crawford. "I'll make it worth your while."

"No need to do any more than you've done coming down here. The same amount will be fine with me and Tommy," he said as he looked at Tommy. Tommy nodded his head.

"Thanks again," said Crawford. "I'm gonna take off now. I gotta few more hours of daylight and here's a letter that I wrote giving you the authority to move the three hundred head to Ft. Worth."

"Thank you, Mr. Crawford and I hope Buster is okay by the time you get there."

Tommy spoke up without even thinking, "And he'll be in our prayers." The shock stunned him as he realized the words just flowed from his mouth. *What's going on*, he was thinking. *I can't seem to stop talking about, or thinking about God.*

Jake looked at Tommy, but said nothing, although he was thinking, *looks like Tommy's got religion, he sounds like his old man.*

Mr. Crawford said his goodbyes to his men and left.

Tommy looked at Jake, and said, "We need to talk."

"So, talk, I'm listening," said Jake.

"Not here," replied Tommy, "can we go outside?"

"Sure!" Jake turned and downed the rest of his drink and followed Tommy outside. "What's goin on Tom?"

Tommy felt nervous but continued, "We've got another wrangler to take with us."

"Wrangler, what do you mean?"

"The girl in the saloon, the younger one, I asked her to join us."

"Are you kidding? The trail is no place for a woman and we've got business to do. How did this happen?"

"It's a long story Jake, but trust me I had no choice in the matter. She needs help, I offered to help, and she accepted. That's all there is."

"Tommy, your young when it comes to women, believe me they all want help."

"Maybe that's true, but I feel obligated to help this one."

"Obligated, what did you two do?"

"Come on Uncle Jake, it isn't like that and I can't explain it all; but it's something I need to do for her. She won't be any trouble, and I'll take care of her."

"She's only going to Ft. Worth, right?"

"I don't know Uncle Jake we'll just have to wait and see."

Jake was thinking over everything that Tommy had said and was feeling a bit upset with him. *How did he get mixed up with a saloon girl? Doesn't he know what she does? And how could he be so taken by this woman when he's got a cute little thing like Molly back home?* "Tommy," Jake said. "There's no way that girl can go with us once we set out after those Mexicans."

"I know that Uncle Jake, but I just felt like I had to help her."

"Okay, on this call, it's all yours, but she's your ward."

"Thanks, Uncle Jake, and you'll see, it'll all work out." Tommy didn't know how it would work out but he believed it would. Somehow he knew it was God's plan all he had to do was follow the plan. The trouble was, he didn't know where the plan led, but he had to follow it. He also didn't know how he knew that, but he did.

"It'd better, and you can quit with the uncle stuff just call me Jake like everyone else."

"Okay... Jake," said Tommy. "And you can call me Tom."

They looked at each other and smiled: they both realized how much they liked each other.

Chapter 9

Early the next morning, Tommy met Cindy in front of the saloon, with the horse and saddle he had bought her. As it turned out, Cindy was able to get a shirt and a pair of jeans from one of the other girls. Tommy thought she looked a lot different now that she didn't have all that make-up on. She was pretty in a plain sort of way; he liked her.

Jake and the other cowboys were waiting at the stable for them. Jake too thought Cindy looked really nice, but she was still one of those girls. "Let's mount up," Jake said. "We need to get that herd movin to Fort Worth."

Once they got to camp and packed up they were ready to go. Jake told Cindy to stay with the chuck wagon and help the cook with cleaning and such. He also pointed out that the cook 'Rascal' was in charge.

The chuck wagon moved ahead of the herd so that dinner could be prepared while they were bringing up the herd, and settling them down. Fort Worth wasn't very far, but it would still take a few days to get there with a slow moving herd.

After a long first day, and supper was over, they were all sitting around the campfire. Smiley picked up his guitar and was playing some of those good old prairie songs. They were all enjoying the music when Tommy said to Cindy, "Why don't you sing us a song?"

The rest of the cowhands joined in asking Cindy to sing.

"Thanks Tommy and the rest of you gentleman, for askin. Hum, let's see." she said. "Maybe," she spoke to Smiley, "You know this one." She began to sing and Smiley figured out the key she was in, and started to strum the guitar in the background.

The rest of the men sat there enjoying the warmth of the fire and her singing to them. She was a rather attractive girl and everyone noticed. Jake too felt the attraction. It had been a long time since he had thought about a woman. She was a woman that was for sure. But, she was a saloon girl. He wondered how many men she had known. He also wondered what would cause an attractive woman to end up in a saloon. Why was she there? He also wondered how Tommy got involve with this woman; and what was the story between the two of them. These were all questions he wondered about, but he knew he would never ask. He believed that people were what they wanted to be; although sometime fate moves you in a direction you don't want do go. He certainly would not be a gunfighter except for fate. Maybe that's what happened to her, fate.

Eduardo and his men had set up camp in the valley between Abilene and Wichita Falls. Then they began to attack and rob the stagecoaches on these trails; first one and then the other. Eduardo knew that it wouldn't take long for the authorities to figure out that they were camped somewhere between these two cities. His plan was to hit both Abilene, and Wichita Falls stagecoaches. This should bring the Cavalry out looking for them. With the Cavalry looking for them he would move closer to Ft. Worth and strike there; then they would go for the bank in Wichita Falls and cross the border into Oklahoma. Once in Oklahoma they would find a quite place to rest before heading back to Mexico. Yes, this new plan seemed good to Eduardo and his men, if they struck hard and fast he might not lose any men. If he could stay ahead of the Cavalry and the Texas Rangers they would be okay.

Unbeknown to them, Jake and Tommy were moving closer and closer to the showdown with Eduardo. The closer they got to Ft. Worth the closer they got to Eduardo. Eduardo's men were headed in the same direction. Neither party knew what the other was doing.

The second night out on the trail, Jake and the men were again resting around the campfire. Cindy was still cleaning up over by the chuck wagon. Jake saw her over there and strolled over. "Hi Cindy," he said. "How do you like life on the trail?"

"It's certainly different than anything I've ever done before, but I like it. It's much better than what I was doing. I really can't thank you and Tommy enough for all that you've done."

"Yea," said Jake. "I suppose anything would be better than what you were doing. If you don't mind me askin, and you don't have to answer; but how did you, or what caused you to start doing that anyway?"

She thought about what he was asking, and really didn't want to talk about it, but she felt obligated. "It was just a series of events, I suppose: I lost my parents, then the farm, all the money was gone, I couldn't get a job except at the saloon. Once you start working in a saloon it's only a matter of time before you give up on life. Once you do that there's really nothing left except how to survive. Had it not been for Tommy, I don't know if I ever would've gotten out of there."

"Tommy's a great guy," he said. "And just so you know, I wouldn't call him Tommy anymore, I'd call him Tom. Only a man would have helped you get out of that life. I'm sure he would appreciate the name change; he's been trying to get me to call him that for awhile. I think now he's earned it."

"Yea, I think your right. I guess I still see him as a kid, I suppose because I'm a little older than he is?"

"I wouldn't think you're much older at least not from this old timer's point of view."

"I don't think you're such an old timer, as you put it, I'd think about thirty-five."

"That's an old timer honey, at least where you're concerned."

"I don't think that's so. You can't tell a real man by his age anyway."

"What do you know about a real man?" said Jake.

"I know a real man by the way they treat a woman. Most men I've met, treat me like a piece of meat. They figure, I am there to devoir and then leave. You and Tommy have treated me better than any man I've ever known. I think your both real men." She thought for a few seconds about Jake, she liked him. "And by the way I'm twenty-six; I just look young for my age."

"You sure do!" said Jake. "It's hard for me to believe you're more than nineteen or twenty years old. It's also hard for me to believe you ever worked in a saloon." There was something about this girl that appealed to him. But she was still a saloon girl that had more experience than he would like to imagine. He was starting to have feelings for this woman that he couldn't understand. *Be careful boy*, he said to himself, *remember where she came from.*

"Perhaps you ought to join the others," she said. "They might get the wrong idea about what your doin over here talkin to me."

"I really don't give a damn what they think. But I guess I ought to join them anyway. I've enjoyed our talk. I hope I haven't embarrassed you in any way."

"Embarrassed me," she said. "That would be a first."

"If you're done here, why don't I walk you back over to the others? We can say goodnight along the way."

"Thanks Jake, I'd like that."

They slowly walked back toward the campfire, but neither was in a hurry, they were feeling comfortable with each other and wondering why.

The U.S. Cavalry, led by Captain Frost, had left Fort Worth in pursuit of the renegade Mexicans. Everyone suspected it was the same group that had been robbing the farmers and rancher. They seemed to have changed what they were doing. All of a sudden they started robbing stagecoaches; they had hit one outside of Abilene, and then another outside of Wichita Falls. Captain Frost believed they must be camped somewhere between the two cities. He headed directly between the two cities. His plan was to circle around to see if they could catch them, or at least find out where they were camping.

He had heard that the Texas Rangers were also closing in; perhaps between the two of them they could catch these desperados. Captain Frost was hoping that the Cavalry caught them before the Texas Rangers. The Texas Rangers would string them up on the spot, but he was hoping to bring them to trial because of all the people they had hurt. It would give the victims a chance at closure if they could face the people who had robbed them. On the other hand, if the Texas Rangers hanged them they would save the cost of a trial; however, it would take a long time for the victims to hear that they had been caught and hung. Perhaps, they would never hear that they had been caught, and if they did, they may never believe it was true.

The herd was nearing Fort Worth and they were camped about two days out. Tommy was practicing his fast draw while Jake and the others watched. Jake was impressed, he was really getting good at getting his gun out. But it would take some time for Jake to teach him how to aim and fire from the hip, time they really didn't have. It would be great if they could have been practicing that too, but Jake couldn't take the chance of spooking the herd with gunshots.

Cindy came over to Jake, who was sitting by the campfire and said, "How about a piece of pie, cowboy?"

Jake looked up at her, *a striking woman for sure*, he thought. "Yea that looks great. When did you have time to bake a pie?"

"I didn't do anything. Rascal baked it while we were eating supper. I was going to have a piece and thought you'd like one too."

Then he noticed she was holding two pieces, "Very thoughtful of you. Would you like to sit down?"

"Don't mind if I do." She said.

Jake looked her over as she moved to sit down, *She sure fills those jeans out nice*, he thought. He could feel his heart begin to beat a little harder as he began to think about her. It had been a long time since he had been with a woman, but just like riding a horse, sometimes your thoughts need to be reined in.

"You know," he said, "I can't think of having a better time on a cattle drive, that is, since you've joined us." He took a bite of his pie and began to chew.

"That's nice to hear," she said. "I would say the same thing, but I've never been on a cattle drive." She began to eat her pie as she looked at him and smiled. He was really a handsome man, rugged and strong and something else about him she couldn't quite figure out. She felt really comfortable with him, he made her feel safe.

She has a pretty smile, he thought to himself. "Cindy, I think I should tell you something. It seems that I'm beginning to take a fancy to you and I know that's not a good thing. For one thing, I know I'm too old and for another I'm a man without a home. You probably don't feel the same way about me, I know, but I do know you like me. I just thought I should tell you how I feel, you can do with it what you want. I just thought you ought to know."

She looked at him for awhile sizing him up then she thought to herself, *I really don't think he's too old, and I'm without a home too; but I do feel safe with this man, and I need safe.*

"Jake," she said. "I want to be honest with you. I've got a lot of wear and tear on me for my age, and I've been around too many men, but I've never met anyone like you. I've only known you for a few days, but I certainly have feeling for you too. As far as age is concerned, it doesn't matter to me, and anyway, I don't think you're that old. I too have no home, but I feel safe with you, and let me tell you a girl needs to feel safe. It doesn't matter to me whether were here on the trail or living in a house, if we both feel good about each other, we could be happy. I think, I would like to take care of you. I think you're a good man Jake, and I think we could be happy."

Take care of me, he thought. *A man always takes care of a woman; or maybe not. He thought about life on a farm and how everyone had to do their own chores. I guess they should take care of each other.* "Why don't we see how the rest of this trip works out for us? I don't know if you know it or not, but Tom and I are after the men who killed his folks. His father was my brother, and he was a preacher and a good man, nobody should have killed him. Tom and I won't rest until we catch up to those murderin thieves."

"No," she said. "I didn't know that. But, Tommy's father being a preacher sure tells me something about him."

"What do you mean?"

"Well, back at the saloon Tommy started to tell me all about God and how much God loved me. It shocked me at first but then he was saying words that I needed to hear. I couldn't understand how he knew that God loved me, but if his father was a preacher, he ought to know."

Wow, that was a surprise for Jake to hear. Tommy was hell bent on catching those men who killed his father and mother. But now he wondered what Tommy's father would say? If he knew his brother, he would be telling them to forgive those guys. Sometimes, he thought, his brother was an idiot, but then, he had to admit he was one of the best men he had ever known. He was always there with words of comfort for everybody; looks like his kid is following in his father's footsteps. Tommy may very well have changed Cindy's life and maybe his too. Time would tell.

He wondered if Tommy could really shoot anybody let alone kill them. If he had anything to do with it he would prevent that from happening. He didn't want Tommy to live the life he was living. When you're always on the move, and never feel safe in any town, you can be the loneliest person in the world; even when you're surrounded by people. It would be a good thing if Tommy became a preacher like his old man. He had the makings of a good one, especially after what he heard Cindy say.

"So, the boy's taken after his old man, eh," Jake said. "Well good for him."

"Yea," said Cindy. "Good for him... He sure came along at the right time in my life."

"Cindy, about everything we've been talkin about, I want you to know, that I really do care for you; but I don't know how we could make it together. We'll just have to wait and see."

"Jake, my father taught me how to use a rifle, and I'm not a bad shot; maybe you could teach me how to use a six-gun, then, I could watch your back."

"You're thinking about riding along with me and wearing britches the rest of your life; or traveling who knows where in order to stay one step ahead of someone who's looking for you; of never having a home or kids or a place to call your own."

"Jake, that's the life I've been living. What's wrong with riding together? I haven't thought of a home in a long time and certainly not children. And what if we only stayed together for a few years, and then I decided that those things were something I really didn't want. If we parted then, at least we would have a few years together. For now, I'm willing to settle for that."

"You're a remarkable woman Cindy. I've never heard a woman talk that way before. But how can you be so certain that's what you want to do. I mean it's a big step to travel with a man especially one that is known as a gunfighter; and I can't even imagine you shooting someone to protect me."

"Why not, I think you would do that for me. What's wrong with me doing it for you?"

"Women just don't use a gun that way."

"Desperate times call for desperate measures."

His brain was on overload. He couldn't believe what she was saying. How could any woman give up everything to be a saddle tramp? Then he began to think, *this is something that could work. I could teach her to use a gun and no one would suspect a woman could use one. And with her background she might just pull the trigger. It sure would be good to have her with me.* He began to think of camping out together and his lonely nights would be filled with so much more. The more he listened to her talk the more he became convinced this could work.

"Cindy, you are an exciting woman to say the least. You really make me feel like a man; a man who really needs taken care of. If you're willing to give it a try, I'm willing too."

Cindy put her plate down and quickly sprang up throwing herself into his arms. As she kissed him she said, "You won't be sorry Jake. I promise you won't be sorry."

Jake was stunned. He just sat there for a few minutes feeling her lips on his not knowing how to react. Then he slowly lifted his arms around her and kissed her back. *Holy cow,* he thought. *This woman is full of surprises.* But he liked what he saw and felt.

Chapter 10

Captain Frost and the Cavalry found the place where the renegade Mexicans had camped. Since there was no one there they had to believe they had moved on, but what direction. He had his scout look for the trail marks to see which way they went.

As the Cavalry moved around the campsite, high up on the ridge Eduardo and his men were watching from cover. They had left a trail heading northward until they came to a rocky trail that would leave no horse prints. There they had put bags on the horse's hoofs to prevent them from leaving a trail. Then they doubled back to where they were now to see if it worked. They were watching the Cavalry when the scout called to the Captain and pointed at the trail. It had worked they were heading northward following the trail.

Eduardo was proud of himself. He was a clever man he thought. Now that the Cavalry was away from Ft. Worth they could hit the stage on that route and then head to Wichita Falls. They would still have a garrison of soldiers there but they would not be able to come after them. With the patrol out they would have to stay there and guard the Fort. All they had to do was scout the trail and watch for the Rangers. Eduardo and his men mounted up and headed for Fort Worth.

Jake was leading the herd into the coral at Fort Worth while the soldiers there were helping. Three hundred head of cattle would feed the soldiers at Fort Worth as well as the community that had developed outside the fort. The little community was a city also known as Fort Worth, Texas. It was a small city at that time, but it had the usual establishments: a bank, a store, a livery stable and a sheriff. It was loosely made up of about two hundred or more people. The farms surrounded the Fort; in times of trouble they could all head for the Fort.

When the cattle had all been corralled, and Jake had received the money for them, they headed to the nearest saloon. Pay day was always a day of celebration. Jake had taken out the money for him and Tom and gave the rest to Lefty, who would be taking it back to Mr. Crawford. All of this had been previously arranged between him and Crawford.

In the morning, he and Tom would be going after the Mexicans. He would check with the local sheriff to see if they had any leads. But tonight was celebration. The herd had been delivered and Jake had found himself a lady. They all went to the saloon for a drink. Cindy came with them, although Jake was concerned. Women didn't wear pants too often, and he wasn't sure how she would be accepted, but it was her call.

As they stood at the bar one of the men recognized Cindy, "Hi honey," he said. "Haven't I seen you at the Lazy Day Saloon, over in Dallas?"

Jake's ears perked up. Cindy stood between him and the man. The guy was huge. Jake was six foot tall but this guy was probably about five inches taller. Jake said, "Excuse me partner, but the lady is with me."

"I didn't mean anything by it mister, if she's with you. But I'm pretty sure she worked at the saloon over in Dallas."

"What difference does that make? I told you she was with me and that's all that needs to be said."

"Well, maybe it is and maybe it isn't. Why don't you let her speak for herself?"

Jake stepped out away from the bar to stand in front of Cindy.

"Wait a minute," said Cindy, "You guys don't have to make a fuss over me. And you're right mister, I can speak for myself. I did work at the saloon in Dallas, but I don't anymore, does that answer your question?"

"Hey, that's all I was askin," said the man. But he was looking at Jake who had stepped away from the bar, and was standing in front of him. "If I was you mister," he said, "I'd take this woman, and leave this saloon."

"You ain't me," said Jake. "Do you have a problem with us staying here?"

"I wouldn't have mister, but you're standing in front of me. Where I come from, that's a challenge, and nobody challenges Big Mike."

"And nobody challenges me either, or talks down to a lady I'm with," Jake said. "The way I see it, you can apologies to the lady, and then 'you' can leave the saloon."

"Come on," said Cindy. "I told you both to quit makin a fuss over me. Let me buy you both a drink."

"Too late for drinks," said the big man.

Jake saw the fist coming: it was moving rapidly from his left. He lifted his left arm to block it, but the power of that punch knocked his arm aside and drove into his head. He felt the explosion as though he had been kicked by a horse. He sailed backward about ten feet spinning around as he fell face down on a table, turning it over. He was dazed from the blow; all he could see was stars spinning around in his head. He tried to get up, but he had no strength. He was aware of hands on his shoulders dragging him to his feet and turning him around. He opened his eyes just in time to see the fist coming straight at his eye. He was conscious enough to drop to his right knee barely missing the punch that he felt breeze over his head. He looked up at the big man as he quickly, with his left hand, grabbed a hold of the big man's belt buckle. While holding his belt buckle with his left, he drove his right fist as hard as he could between the big man's legs. He heard a loud roar from above him as the big man yelled. While still holding his belt buckle, he drove several more punches, in rapid succession, into his private parts. The big man began to howl, and slowly sank to his knees holding himself.

As quickly as Jake could he got up from the floor. He knew he couldn't fight this guy, nor could he give him a chance; so he stepped back with his right leg, and with all the force he could muster he drove his right foot under his chin knocking him backward onto the floor. Then he stumbled forward over the man who was still moaning; he drew his knee up to his chest and turned while stomping downward driving his boot-heal into the side of the big man's head. His head bounced off the floor, and he was knocked unconscious.

Jake turned around to see where Cindy was. Standing next to her were two men who had come in with the big man. Both men reached for their guns. But by instinct, in a flash, Jake had pulled his gun and was pointing it at the two men before they could clear leather. He was crouched down holding his gun forward with his right hand; his left hand was above the hammer. Both men stood there with their guns half way out to their holsters, mouths open in surprise and fear. Surprise, because they had never seen anyone clear leather that fast; and fear, because both men knew they were dead.

Jake looked at them with death in his eyes and said, "Don't make me kill you!"

Anyone else would have shot them and not taken any chances. But that was Jake. He never knew when he drew his gun if he would be faster; but once he had the drop on someone there was no need to shoot unless they continued to draw. He was happy that they didn't draw. Tomorrow they would be happy that they didn't draw.

"Drop your guns on the floor, and do it slowly," Jake said while still holding that menacing stare. When they hesitated to move, he yelled through gritted teeth, "Now!"

Both men jumped and slowly took their guns from their holsters and dropped them on the floor.

"Now you two get your friend and get him out of here."

"What about our guns?" one of them said.

"The bartender will keep your guns until tomorrow," Jake said as he looked at the bartender. The bartender nodded his head. Jake squatted down and took the big man's gun from his holster, and then he motioned with his gun to the two men to move.

He stood there holding his gun looking around the room watching them as they took their friend out the swinging doors.

Alongside of Cindy stood Tommy; both guns drawn, he too looked around the room trying to cover his uncle Jake. They were both waiting to see if anyone else was going to interfere. Jake felt good knowing that Tommy had his back; in this entire ruckus he had forgotten about him.

The swinging doors opened again and another big man entered the room. He wasn't as tall as the other man but he was big in stature and he wore a badge. He was Sheriff Brown. "What's goin on here," he said. He looked around the room and at the two men standing there with their guns drawn. "You boy's can put up the guns, we don't want any trouble. Just tell me what's goin on."

Jake and Tommy put their guns away but Jake spoke first, "It was just a misunderstanding Sheriff. I think everything is okay now." He looked around the room to make sure.

"Just a misunderstanding huh!" said the Sheriff. "Henry" he said to the bartender, "Can you tell me what happened?"

"Sure Sheriff," said Henry. "Big Mike come in here messin with that lady there" he pointed at Cindy. "The guy over there told him to apologize and Big Mike hit him. As it turned out that guy beat up Big Mike and made Jesse and Butch carry him out. That's all there was to it Sheriff."

"What's your name big fellah," he asked as he looked at Jake.

"Jake Wade"

The room really got quite now.

"Jake Wade, I think we heard of you. How come you never killed those boys?"

"I never kill anyone unless I have to Sheriff," Jake replied.

"The only thing I know about you is that a lot of dead men have met you. How come you let those boys go?"

"I told you Sheriff, there wasn't any need to shoot anybody. Those boys agreed with me, so I didn't have to do any shootin."

The sheriff stood there looking at Jake. He didn't seem to be afraid at all. "What's your business here in Fort Worth?"

"We brought that herd of cattle in today. We plan on leavin tomorrow or the next day and headin back to Oklahoma."

"Tomorrow or the next day sounds good, but I don't want no shootin in my town, okay."

"That's fine with me Sheriff, we don't want any trouble."

"Okay," said the sheriff as he looked around the bar at everyone, "You folks have a good night tonight. I'm gonna go find Big Mike and have a talk with him." With that he turned and walked out the door.

They did have a good time that night and there wasn't any more trouble. Big Mike never came back and everyone was glad.

The next day Eduardo and his men held up the stagecoach just outside of Fort Worth. They got the strong box and the money that was inside. The guard was shot but he was still alive. The Mexicans headed south away from the stagecoach so the people could see which way they were going. After a few miles they turned northward towards Wichita Falls. The plan was working just as Eduardo thought it would.

The stagecoach came limping into town about 3:00 in the afternoon. There was a lot of commotion about what had happened, and people were standing around trying to decide what to do. The sheriff was putting together a posse to go after them when Jake and Tommy came up.

"What's going on Sheriff?" Jake asked.

"Stagecoach has been robbed. I'm puttin together a posse to get them. Do you want to go with us?"

"I don't think it's my problem Sheriff. Do you have any idea who the robber's were?"

"The driver said it was about eight Mexicans. He said they were a mean bunch and thought they were all going to get killed."

"Mexicans," Jake asked as he looked at Tommy. "Any better identification there's a lot of Mexicans around."

"Yea," said the Sheriff. "The leader was dressed in black; we think he was Eduardo. He leads a small band of Mexican's that have been robbing farmers and ranchers, but now it seems their robbing stagecoaches. The Cavalry's after them as well as the Texas Ranger but they haven't been caught yet. Are you sure you don't want to help out. We could sure use your gun."

"When you plannin on leavin Sheriff?"

"Probably not till morning the sun's goin down soon. We'll do better in the morning when we can see what we're doing. Plus, I need to get a few men deputized. If you want to go with us meet me at the Sheriff's office at 8:00 in the morning."

"Okay Sheriff," said Jake. "We'll talk it over and let you know."

On the way back to the hotel, Jake and Tommy talked about whether they should go with the posse or not. The main thing was to get these guys once and for all. If riding with the sheriff was the way to do it; it would work for them. Jake had decided that Cindy should go back north with Rascal and the chuck wagon to Crawford's ranch. He and Tommy would meet her there and then go back to Chickasha. All he needed to do was to convince her to go there and wait for him.

When they went into the hotel lobby, Cindy was sitting on the couch waiting for them. Jake walked over and sat down beside her.

Jake began, "Cindy the men that Tommy and I are after have just held up the stagecoach. The sheriff and the posse are going after them in the morning. He asked Tommy and me to go with them. We decided to go with them because we need to make sure these guys get caught. Do you understand?"

"Yes," said Cindy. "I won't be any trouble. I'll stay out of the way."

"That's not what I had in mind," he said. "This is not the same as you and me traveling together. This is going to lead to a shoot-out and these men are very dangerous. I don't want you to get hurt."

"I don't want you to get hurt either," she said. "I don't care how dangerous it is, I want to be with you. If it comes to a shoot out, I'll have my rifle, and I can stay a way off."

"That's not going to work. If you go, I'll be worrying about you, and that could put my life in danger. After you learn to aim and fire a side arm it will be different, but it will take you time to learn."

"If you're going to worry about me now, then you will worry about me later, so we may as well call the whole thing off."

"Whoa... wait a minute honey," Jake said. "Let's not get caught up in this thing now and think that I'm trying to back out on what I said. That's not the case at all. We'll be riden hard and long so believe me when I say this is no place for a woman."

"Jake you're impossible. If you don't want me to go now, then you won't want me to go later either."

"Please Cindy hear me out, Okay."

"Okay," she said.

"What I have in mind is for you to go back to Oklahoma with Rascal and the chuck wagon to Mr. Crawford's ranch. He's a pretty good friend of mine and I'm sure you can stay with him until Tommy and I come for you. We can meet you there and then go on to Chickasha where Tommy lives. Once there we can work on your shooting skills and get ready for the trail together. Once we start out together we will stay together from then on I promise no matter what."

"I don't know Jake. It isn't what I had in mind the other times we talked."

"I know Cindy. But you remember last night at the saloon when I got in the fight with the big guy and his two friends tried to draw against me?"

"Yes."

"Well that would have been a case of self defense. If I would have shot them they would be dead and I would have someone else's family looking for me. Situations like that you can't control. But this posse is going after some pretty bad outlaws that are cold-blooded killers; and those guys's wouldn't think anything about killing you. I couldn't have that on my conscience: I care too much for you. Please be patient and do what I ask this time."

She sat there thinking over what he had said. She had planned on them being together from now on. She couldn't believe she could care so much about someone she just met a week ago. "Okay." she said, "but please be careful and come get me as soon as you can. I'll wait."

"Thanks honey," he said as he put his arm around her and pulled her to him. He held her there for a few minutes. He wanted to kiss her but you didn't do things like that in public. "I promise I won't be any longer than it takes and then it will be you and me always, all right?"

"All right," she said. "But it's not going to be easy waiting for you so you'd better hurry."

"I promise once we get these bandits, I'll put my horse to the sweat in order to get to you."

She held on to him for a while then said, "We have tonight."

"Do you mean what I think you mean?"

"Not exactly, if this was last week, then maybe; but when I talked of a new beginning I mean a new beginning. I can't go back to what I was before, not even for you. I really believe Tommy was right. God really does love me and I love him and I want to be what He wants me to be. So if I do anything with you now I'll be no different than what I was in Dallas. Do you understand?"

"I think so," said Jake. "But it really doesn't make sense. What did you think was going to happen before we hit the trail, we were gonna get married or something?"

"I hadn't thought much about that. I guess, we'll have to wait and see what happens," she said.

"You women sure make it hard on a man," said Jake.

"If you think it's hard for you then just think how hard it is for me. You're going to be occupied with catching those men so you won't be thinking much about me. But I'm going to be headed up north to a place I've never been before with a grumpy old cook. I'll have nothing to do but think about you."

"Well, I wouldn't say that I won't be thinking about you. I've never thought of a woman so much in my life as I've thought about you this past week. Believe me honey, now that I know you, the last thing I want to do is leave you."

She liked it when he called her honey. It made her feel warm and secure. But she was going to miss him terribly. "Thanks Jake," she said. "What shall we do tonight?"

They ended up going back to the saloon for the late show. It wasn't great but it was something to do and they were together.

Early the next morning Cindy left with Rascal and the other ranch hands; they were heading for Crawford's ranch in Oklahoma. Jake and Tommy joined the posse and headed out looking for Eduardo and his men. Four days out they ran into Captain Frost and the Cavalry.

Captain Frost spoke to the sheriff who informed him that the Mexicans had robbed the stagecoach near Fort Worth. Captain Frost had not heard about the stagecoach robbery, but he assured the Sheriff that the Mexicans were nowhere in the plains between Wichita Falls and Abilene. He didn't know if they had headed north or south but if they hit the stagecoach near Fort Worth then they should be somewhere in-between, or maybe on their way back to Mexico. The Captain said he would take his troops and head south if the sheriff wanted to head north that way they should be able to find them. They agreed.

Then the sheriff asked Captain Frost, "What about the Texas Rangers?"

"I haven't heard anything about them," said the Captain. "I can only suppose their looking too. You know them; there a fearsome bunch of lawmen. You may run into them; if you do tell them about our plan. They may have some other ideas of their own."

"I will," said the sheriff. He took his men and headed north towards Wichita Falls.

They had been riding for several hours. Jake was wondering what he would do if he were this Mexican. *For quite a few years he had been robbing farmers and ranchers, and now he suddenly changes to robbing stagecoaches. Why would he do that?* He thought. *He would take the farmer's livestock and sell them in the next town. If he robbed the same people or people who lived close by, and sold their livestock to the people of the next town; the town's people would eventually recognize him, and he could no longer sell their livestock without being recognized. Hum*, he thought.

The last farm he hit was down around Del Reo, which is in the far south of Texas. Then he robs a stagecoach near Wichita Falls, and then Abilene, and now Fort Worth. These three cities are all in the northern part of Texas. It seems like he's working his way north, but north to where, to Oklahoma? 'Oklahoma', my God, he thought, that's where he killed Tommy's parents and my brother. On the way to Oklahoma, from here, is Wichita Falls. Could it be that he's planning on robbing another stagecoach near Wichita Falls? No this would be too soon, he thought.

What if he's planning on robbing the bank at Wichita Falls? It's a pretty big step from robbing stagecoaches to robbing banks. But he's changed what he did before, so this could be another change. As a matter of fact, he thought, *what if the stagecoach robberies were a decoy to what he was really planning. If, I was this Eduardo and needed money, I'd go after the bank at Wichita Falls. He had to share this idea with the Sheriff and see what he thought.*

Jake rode up to the sheriff and told him they needed to stop for a few minutes, so that they could talk. The sheriff agreed because they needed a rest anyway. Jake shared his thoughts with the sheriff who agreed that it did sound logical. But, by the time they got to Wichita Falls, he might have already been there and gone.

"That might be true Sheriff," said Jake. "But I think we ought to head directly to Wichita Falls. If we burn leather we might get there in time to prevent a robbery, and catch a thief."

"Sounds like a good idea to me," said the sheriff. They mounted up and took off for Wichita Falls as fast as their horses could go.

Chapter 11

Eduardo had sent two of his men into Wichita Falls to look things over. In 1885 Wichita Falls was a thriving city that covered a good two miles long and two miles wide. Because of the businesses in the city, the bank would be loaded. They had reported to him that the sheriff had taken a posse out of town to look for them. It looked like the bank was almost unprotected. The problem was, that the bank was in the heart of town. This meant they would have to ride one mile into town to get to the bank, and then ride one more mile to get out of town. The Oklahoma boarder was only a day's ride north from there. The distance could be covered in less time if you really were riding. This was going to be harder than Eduardo thought. The only good thing was that the sheriff was out of town, and he couldn't cross the border into Oklahoma. So if they were able to get out of town with the money they might be able to get away. Life was full of risks, he and his men had been taking them for years, and so far the odds had been in their favor.

The question was, should they wait until the bank closed, or should they brake in? If they did how would they open the safe; or what time of day should they hit the bank? Eduardo was thinking this one through because they had never robbed a bank and didn't know what to expect. He figured that early in the morning might be a good idea. The bank opened at 9:00 a.m. and they could be waiting for it to open; it would be better than the afternoon because people might not be that alert. They could ride into town early in the morning and find cover near the bank and wait. So he had decided that it would be 9:00 tomorrow morning.

The sheriff of Wichita Falls had taken a posse of about twenty men and rode out to town two days ago, because of news that he received by telegram. But they camped just outside of town. The sheriff was a pretty smart man who had been a good sheriff for the past few years. He stayed alive because he was a thinking man. He only used his gun if it was the last resort.

The news that he received by telegram followed one he had received a few days before. It said that a band of Mexican had held up the stagecoach near Fort Worth. That followed the one that he had received that said the same thing about Abilene. The sheriff figured that the Mexicans, first hit the stagecoach at Wichita Falls, then the one near Abilene. He thought surely they were headed south back to Mexico, until he received the telegram from Fort Worth. This didn't make any sense to him; he would have to talk this over with his men.

As they sat at camp the sheriff began to tell the men of his suspicions. "Men, I gotta run something by you to see what you think. So let me finish what I need to say, and then you can tell me your ideas, okay?" They all nodded their heads, and some said a brief, yes.

"Well," he said, "this band of Mexicans, isn't making any sense to me. They first rob the stagecoach her in Wichita Falls, then a few days later they rob the stagecoach near Abilene. I figured that made sense since they were on their way back to Mexico. Then I get this telegram that they robbed the stagecoach at Fort Worth. That makes no sense at all to me. Why would they take a chance and rob a stagecoach at Fort Worth, knowing the U.S. Cavalry was there. They're definitely not heading back to Mexico. The only thing that makes sense to me is that their planning on going north, maybe to Oklahoma; that means they'll be coming back this way. What do you all think?"

His main deputy Luke spoke up as he looked around at the others, "That sounds like something I would do if I needed money, and wanted to get out of

Texas fast. I think you're right Sheriff, they may well be headin back this way."

The Sheriff looked around at everybody, "You all agree with me and Luke?"

They all nodded their heads, and some murmured "yes."

"Okay," said the Sheriff. "Here's my plan. I brought you boys out of town in order to set a trap for these bandits. What I want to do is split you up into four groups, of five. This way we can cover the south end of Wichita Falls. If they are comin back here we can cover the road to the south, in case they try to get another stagecoach. If that's not their plan then they might be comin to rob our bank.

If they are planning on robbin our bank, they'll be comin from the south. We can cover the trail about three miles apart, and stay undercover so that you're not seen. That means no fires at night, and no talkin above a whisper; remember sound travels. We got a lot of Mexicans in the area, so what you're lookin for are a couple of strangers that are comin into town. I figure if they're planning on gettin the bank they'll no doubt send in a couple to spy out things. The town will tell everybody that we left in search of the bandits. That's why we're here. If you spot a stranger, you can send one of your men to me with word, and one of your men should tail them and see what they do. Either way, you need to be in touch with me, and report whatever you see."

The Sheriff continued, "If we believe these are the hombres, then we'll sneak back into town after midnight, and take up our positions around the bank, and wait for them, any questions?"

Luke spoke up, "You mean we should sneak back into town so none of the townsfolk know we're there. We're gonna hide from them too?"

"I think you got the picture, Luke. Look boys, if the towns people know we're there they'll be looking at our positions; that will give us away. If we're gonna set a trap, we need to be quiet about it. Do you all understand now?"

Luke said, "Yea, Sheriff, I understand." The rest agreed. It was now just a matter of waiting.

Sure enough the next day, they spotted two Mexican men headed toward the city. They followed them and watched as they checked out the bank. One of the men asked a woman where the sheriff's office was, and she told him the sheriff was out of town; she said he went after the men who robbed the stagecoach. They watched the men leave town, then reported what they had seen to the sheriff. They would have followed the men back to their camp, but they knew Eduardo would have the trail watched. The best way to get them was in the act of robbing the bank. The sheriff assigned their positions placing them on certain roof tops, and windows, near the bank. They rode into town quietly after midnight, two at a time, and took up their position to wait. The trap had been set.

Meanwhile, Sheriff Brown from Fort Worth, with his posse, as well as Jake and Tommy, set up camp for the night. They were a good hard day's ride from Wichita Falls, and still they wouldn't arrive until evening. Jake didn't want to stop but his horse needed the rest, and he knew he had no choice. He could only hope that they would make it there in time. They had no idea what was happening at Wichita Falls, while they were resting.

Early the next morning they broke camp and headed toward Wichita Falls.

At the same time Eduardo and his men had already made their way into town. They were stationed around the bank waiting in the alleys, and doorways, keeping out of sight of the people.

The sheriff was watching from a rooftop, as Eduardo and his men made their way into town. He watched as they hid in the alleys and doorways. Now he had other thoughts on his mind. The bank won't open for another two hours. If he could get word to his men they could attack the bandits before the bank opened, and hopefully prevent more loss of lives. Although, it was quite hard to see in the pale moonlight and it would be harder to hit your target. He would have to wait a little longer for the sun to come up. He looked around the alleyway to see if he could spot the one called Eduardo, but it was too dark. He decided that unless he could get a clear shot at the man in black, he would wait for the bank to open. He had no choice but to wait.

As it turned out Eduardo was well hidden, neither he nor his men were aware that a trap had been set. They were all waiting for the bank to open.

At ten minutes to nine a man unlocked the front door and entered the bank with two other men. Eduardo thought this was the Banker and two tellers. He had already told his men what to do. Three men were to enter the bank and get control of it; then they would open the back door and let him in. With him waiting at the back door he could catch anyone who might try to sneak out. The other four men would ride up on their horses and tie them to the railing. They would wait outside on the porch and make sure he wasn't interrupted. It was a good plan, he thought.

However, the sheriff had switched the banker and the tellers with three of his deputies. They had hidden their guns under their shirts, or stuck them in their boots, it was their choice. Once all of the players were in place, the sheriff would let them know they were surrounded. The deputies inside didn't know the combination to the safe, so Eduardo couldn't rob the bank. His hope was that the three men inside could get the drop on the robbers. The stage was set, all players were in position and it was time to start the game.

The sheriff yelled from a window across the street, "You men on the porch this is the sheriff speaking, you are surrounded, drop your guns and surrender; you are all under arrest."

The four men on the porch were surprised. The sheriff was supposed to be out of town. Who was this? They all went for their guns as they scrambled for cover. The sheriff opened fire and with a single shot from his Winchester he dropped one of the men as he started down the steps.

Everyone started firing their guns. One of the robbers was trying to mount his horse; he never made it. Three shots hit him from different directions, and he fell to the ground dead. Another of the men quickly fell on the street, and rolled under the porch, where he was returning fire at the windows, and rooftops. The other man had jumped down between the horses, and was firing from there. One of the horses to his right was hit, and dropped to the ground, leaving him in the open. He never had a chance to make it under the porch, although he tried; he was hit several times, and fell looking at his friend under the porch. He died within minutes.

Inside of the bank Manuel, Diego and Emilio, had the three men up against a wall. They had let Eduardo in the back door. They told the one they thought was the banker to open the safe, but before they could do anything, they heard the sheriff yell, then all hell broke loose. Eduardo looked out the front window and saw his men scrambling. When he turned around he saw the supposed banker pulling a gun, and he shot him dead. He looked at the other two who were looking over their shoulders at him. "Who has the combination to the safe?" he asked.

Both men looked at the man who was dead on the floor and one of them replied, "He was the only one who had the combination."

"Then," Eduardo said, "Neither one of you are good for anything." Then he put two bullets in each of their backs, and they fell to the floor. Eduardo was furious. How did this happen? He looked at his men. "You two Manuel and Emilio, I thought you said the Sheriff was out to town."

"Si, Señor Eduardo, that's what we were told. Now we are trapped, no?"

"Now we are trapped, Si. I ought to kill you both where you stand."

"But Señor, we can only tell you what we heard. We are trapped to."

"You two," he pointed, "you cover the front door and I'll check the back door."

Eduardo quickly went to the back door and opened it to peek out. Several shots rang out and splinters spit from the door and door post. He quickly closed the door. He went back into the front room of the bank. "Are the hombres outside okay?" he asked.

"We can only hear gunfire from one rifle under the porch Señor" said Manuel. "I think the others, they may be dead."

'Porch' thought Eduardo. *That means there may be a crawl space under the bank.* "Manuel, you and Emilio go upstairs, and see if you can pick anyone off from the windows up there. Diego and me will tear up the floor and see if we can escape that way. Vamoose, and try not to get killed."

Eduardo and Diego began to tear up the floor with a crowbar they found in back while Manuel and Emilio stood off the sheriff and his men upstairs.

It took them a good half hour to tear up the floor and they found the crawl space. Santeago was still alive under the porch and firing at the Sheriff's men. He turned to see Eduardo looking at him from the hole in the floor. They nodded at each other and Santeago turned around and began to fire again.

Eduardo thought this was like old times. He was left with the same four men he had been riding with for the past ten years. Perhaps this was fate. He sent Diego to get Manuel and Emilio. When they were all in the bank they began to open fire out the windows at anything that moved. Then they quickly jumped through the hole in the floor, and began to scramble out the back of the building to where their horses were tied. Eduardo thought there would be someone covering their horses to block their escape. Since he was the best shot he crawled to the back first. He looked out, but to his amazement he saw no one. He motioned for the others to move. They quickly got on their horses, and began to ride, as fast as they could, up the alley away from the bank.

Shots rang out after them and they heard shouting, but they weren't waiting to find out who it was, or what they were saying: they were running for their lives.

The sheriff mounted up his horse with about ten deputies and set pursuit. He left the rest to make sure the others were dead or captured. Eduardo couldn't be more than a mile or two ahead of him and his men. He knew they would be running to the Oklahoma border.

Eduardo and the men with him rode hard until they came to a mountain pass. There Eduardo stopped with his men. "It is time to pay this sheriff back for killing my hombres," he said. "Okay amigos, take cover and let us wait on this posse," said Eduardo. He dismounted and pulled his long rifle from its saddle holster. He was sorry he had not thought to take it inside the bank but he had it now. It was the equalizer. With it he could hit a man almost a mile away.

He was reminded of the soldier he killed to get this rifle. It was truly a marvelous rifle. It had a scope that brought the target up real close. With this he would pick off the sheriff from the top of this pass. The old art of war, *if you kill the leader you cut off the head of the snake, and it no longer knows how to attack.* He would kill the sheriff and the posse would flee.

The sheriff and posse were riding hard strapping their horses trying to overtake Eduardo and his men before they reached the border. They were coming to the mountain pass where he knew Eduardo and his men had already passed. Suddenly, before he heard the sound of the rifle he felt a wall hit his chest, and the pain had a rippling effect on his body. It started in his chest and went throughout his being. He was flying backward off of his horse as he watched it galloping ahead. Then the sudden hit of something hard behind him and he tumbled over and over. He lost consciousness. He was dead.

The posse saw him flying backward off of his horse, and then they heard the sound of a rifle. They all stopped and looked at him. Blood was all over his chest or was that a hole? They couldn't tell from where they sat, but none of them wanted the same fate. They quickly ran for cover behind the rocks. They crouched down there and waited to see if there were any other shots.

Eduardo looked down from his mountain perch. It was a clean shot. The Sheriff would never kill anyone else again. He walked down to his horse and said, "Mount up amigos, we ride for Oklahoma."

The sheriff's posse waited for almost an hour, when no other shots were fired; they figured the Mexicans had left. Slowly, they made their way to the sheriff's body. He was dead.

Chapter 12

Sheriff Brown and his posse rode into Wichita Falls late that afternoon, only to find the people mourning the death of their sheriff. Deputy Luke told them about the attempted bank robbery, and how the sheriff had set a trap to catch them in the bank. "We killed three of them but we think four or five of them got away. We had them dead to right, but two of our men left their post, and allowed them to escape. The sheriff and several men went after them; he was shot with one of them long rifles, and all the others took cover. After a while, when they thought it was safe, they got the sheriff's body and brought it back to town."

The deputy continued, "I stayed here to clean up what was left. I don't know what I would've done, had I been there. The Sheriff was a good man. I don't suppose it will do much good to go after them now. They were headed for Oklahoma, and I'm sure they're there by now."

Jake looked at Tom it was time for them to go alone. The sheriff would have no jurisdiction in Oklahoma it was up to him and Tom now. They said their goodbyes to Sheriff Brown, and Deputy Luke, and headed north.

Eduardo was furious. *That sheriff had out guessed him,* he thought. *How did he know we were going to rob that bank? We were lucky to escape, but we didn't get any money, and our money won't last for long. The stagecoach's weren't carrying that much. The bank would have taken care of us for a long time. We could have returned to Mexico and lived the good life. The sheriff had outguessed me all right but he would never outguess anyone else.* That was one man that he was glad that he killed.

As they continued north toward Fort Sill, Eduardo was concerned about the soldiers there. The telegraph was making it impossible for him to continue in Oklahoma and Texas. He knew that he needed to get back to the safety of Mexico, but they couldn't go back empty handed.

He was thinking about where they might get some money. He wasn't that familiar with Oklahoma, and he had only been in the southern part. He knew that this trail would lead to Fort Sill, and eventually to Oklahoma City. However, it would be very dangerous for them to go to such a big city. In the smaller cities most people kept their money at home. This brought him back to what they used to do before the stagecoaches, and the bank. This time, however, it wouldn't be as prosperous for him and his men; they wouldn't be able to take livestock and sell it. Wherever they went they would have to rob farmers or ranchers or an occasional stagecoach.

He had terrorized this part of Oklahoma last year so he knew the soldiers would be looking for him. They would have to go around Fort Sill, and avoid meeting any Cavalry patrols. The Indian's had not been a problem for the past few years except for the renegade Geronimo. But he was living in New Mexico or Arizona he only came here for raids, so he would have to avoid any Indian parties they might run into.

Life is not getting any easier, he thought. *I need a place to stop and rest, a place where no one would think we were.* His mind scanned the area as best he could and then he thought of something. *The gringo and his wife I killed up here last year,* he thought. *Where was that? Maybe that farm is vacant, if so we could hide out there for awhile. What was the name of that city? It was something about a chicken. Chickchick...no! Chickshane...no! It was an Indian name.* He couldn't remember. He must be getting old he thought. He remembered the name a few days ago, but now his mind was blank.

As they rode along he turned to Manuel and said, "Manuel, remember the gringo and his wife I shot up here last year?"

"Si," said Manuel. The others also nodded their heads. They all remembered because it wasn't like Eduardo to kill a pretty Señora like that one. She was very pretty and Eduardo shot her before they could have any fun with her. Yes they all remembered her.

"What was the name of that city?" said Eduardo.

His men studied the question trying to remember and Emilio said, "Ah, I remember Eduardo, it was an Indian name I think Chickasha."

"Si, Chickasha," said Eduardo. "Si, I think we shall go back to that farm and see if anyone else is living there."

"Si Señor," said all of his men.

Eduardo looked ahead of them and said, "We shall need to get off this trail now that we are coming to the Fort. We will ride west around the Fort and then north to... what was the name of that city Emilio?"

They all replied, "Chickasha."

"Ah, Si, Chickasha," said Eduardo.

Jake and Tommy were nearing the Handlebar Ranch where Cindy was waiting for them. The Handlebar Ranch was just east of the trail that led to Fort Sill, and then to Chickasha. Jake and Tommy had not found Eduardo, but they knew that he was in the area. Jake didn't feel that it was safe for Cindy to travel with them; but he told her he would pick her up on the way to Chickasha. Anyway, he couldn't wait to see her.

As they came near the main house on the ranch; he spotted her coming out of the house. His heart took a leap. He couldn't wait to hold her. He had never felt like this about a woman before. And *she was a Saloon girl*, he thought. *There I go again, will I ever quit thinking about her that way?* But as he looked at her, now running toward him, he knew he couldn't care less where she came from, or what she had done before. She was his woman. He jumped from the horse and grabbed her up in his arms.

Tommy was surprised. He wasn't expecting his uncle Jake to react like that. He hadn't said much to him about her, and there he was making a fool of himself in front of Mr. Crawford and his men.

Jake squeezed her to him as he kissed her check. Then he pushed her away from him by her shoulders so he could look at her. *She was beautiful*, he thought. Her eyes were aglow. His heart was beating so fast, and he had missed her so much, that he couldn't help himself. He pulled her into his arms and kissed her right on the lips. He didn't care who saw what. He was a man and she was his woman. He was so happy that he couldn't resist that kiss.

Cindy too was surprise. She couldn't wait to see him, and when she did, she couldn't stop her feet from running. *Oh God, I hope he's as glad to see me, as I am to see him*, she was thinking. But the question was answered when Jake dismounted his horse and grabbed her up in his arms. She felt his mouth on her cheek and her heart beat faster. He pushed her away and looked at her as she looked at him. She wanted to kiss him so bad but it wasn't proper for a lady to kiss a man in public. But then he pulled her to him and answered all of her questions and desires as he kissed her.

Mr. Crawford, and the others, stood there looking at them, and then at each other. They knew that Jake and Cindy had hit it off while they were on the trail to Fort Worth, but they never knew this. Surely some of them were thinking as Jake had thought, *she was a saloon girl*, but they knew better than to say it. Plus, they all liked Jake and Cindy too, for that matter.

As Tommy watched Jake and Cindy kiss, he couldn't help but think of Molly. Is that the kind of thing that she would want: a man just grabbing a girl and kissing her? He wished she was here to see this; and then thought that if she was, they might be doing the same thing.

When Jake and Cindy parted his face turned red because he realized what he had done. He looked around and took a deep breath, with a notable gulp, and then he looked at Cindy. She was still aglow. *God she's beautiful*, he thought again. He wanted desperately to kiss her again, but this time he controlled his emotions. But it was hard for him to take his eyes off of her.

Finally, Jake turned and faced Crawford, "How's Buster," he said.

"He's doin fine now," he said. "I want to tell you that Cindy here has been fidgeting around here for day's waitin for you to get here. Now I know why?" he laughed.

Cindy's face turned red as she looked down at the ground. She was so glad that Jake still had his arm around her. She felt so secure this way that she wanted to stay like that forever. She couldn't believe what God had done for her. Tommy was right. God loved her and answered her prayer, and she wasn't even a Christian; but she knew in her heart that she wanted to be. She thought, at her first opportunity, she would ask Tommy what she should do to become one.

They all shook hands and greeted each other as they walked into the house. They had some things to talk about. They discussed Eduardo and his men. Jake knew they were somewhere north of where they were now. He knew they would have bypassed the Fort, and continued north; that would leave Chickasha in their path. Jake knew they would have to make hast to Chickasha first thing in the morning. He was wondering if Cindy would wait here for him. It could be dangerous for her if she came along; but in the end it would have to be her call.

That evening after supper Cindy asked Tommy if she could talk to him alone. They quietly left the others and walked out toward the stable. Jake noticed them leaving but, said nothing; however, he was wondering what she wanted to talk to Tommy about.

When they got to the stable, Cindy asked Tommy the question that had been burning in her heart. She had never thought of God in the way she had this past week. She needed some answers, and a preacher's son should know. She bit her bottom lip and then asked, "Tommy, how does someone become a Christian?"

Tommy looked at her and thought, *Oh no, I don't want to talk about God again. What should I tell her,* he thought, *that I don't want to talk about God?* He felt trapped, because she wanted to know, and he did have some answers. He just didn't want to talk about God. He was still angry with God, because of his parents. Now he was angry, because she had asked this question. "Well," he said. "It's really a matter of who you believe in. To be a Christian you must believe in Jesus that makes you a follower of Christ, which makes you a Christian."

"You mean, all I have to do is believe in Jesus, and I'm a Christian?"

"Well, there's a little more to it than that," he said. He still didn't want to talk about God.

"Like what," she asked.

Oh man, here I go again, he thought. *How do I tell her when I don't want to talk? God,* he began to pray unconsciously. *How could you let this happen when you know how I feel?* However, he looked at Cindy and he could see how sincere she was, and also how hungry she was to know the answer. He had no choice. *What would Pa say to her?* He thought.

"Cindy, I could go into a long talk about where sin came from, and that we're all sinners; but the truth is, all that may be true, but God loves us in spite of who we are, or what we've done. You know that what you were doin in that saloon was not right, and to God that is sin. The Bible says, 'when we know to do what is right and we don't do it, it is a sin,' I know it says something like that."

"Well, I knew what I was doin was wrong, but I didn't feel like I had any choice; that is, until you came along."

"But that's what happens to us in life, Cindy. We get caught up in living and forget all about values. You forgot about values but God never forgot about you. If there is anything you can do to be a Christian it's to realize that God loves you no matter what. And He loved us so much that he sent His son Jesus to tell us about that love. The simple answer is this; to be a Christian you just need to accept the forgiveness that God offers through His son."

"But I feel like I already did that Tommy. I mean, I feel so different inside, and I've never thought that much about God until our conversation in the Lazy Day Saloon. I mean, I feel forgiven, I feel so clean, I can't explain it, but I do love God. I want to live the rest of my life for him."

"Do you believe in Jesus?"

"I don't know. I've never heard that much about him. Is it more important to believe in Jesus, than it is to believe in God?"

"Actually, their one and the same, and I don't have time to go into all of this tonight. But let me tell you that you need to read the Bible. When you read the Bible, God will talk to you and you will learn about Him. Do you have a Bible?"

"No," She said.

He stood there thinking for a minute and remembered that he had his Bible in his saddlebag. "Wait here a minute," he said. He walked over to the coral where his horse and saddle were. His saddlebag was on the back of the saddle. He got out his Bible and handed it to her. "Here," he said. "Now you've got no reason not to read."

"But I can't take your Bible. What will you read?"

He wasn't really planning on reading the Bible again, but if he changed his mind, he could get another one. He felt it was important to give his Bible to her. So he did.

"I'll pick one up in Chickasha," he answered.

"Are you sure you don't mind?"

"I'm sure Cindy," he said. Then he realized how good he felt. It was just like he felt in the saloon after he had spoken to her. He felt so much joy that he had to struggle to hold back the tears. *God*, he said to himself. *I'm not worthy to be used by you. I keep struggling not to be used, and you keep using me. And I know, I can feel in my heart that you want me to forgive, but I can't...* Then he wrestled with what he had just said. *Help me God, to forgive.*

Cindy too felt good. She kept looking at the Bible in her hand all the way back to the house. She couldn't wait to open it and begin to read. She wondered what she would find out in this book.

In the house, Jake was telling Crawford that he and Tommy were going after those Mexicans. He had an idea where they might be going, but he was afraid they might decide to stop in Chickasha. He was also afraid that the McGregor's were in danger. They would be leaving first thing in the morning, and go directly to the McGregor's farm to make sure they were okay. From there they would head into Chickasha, and check it out. The rest of his plan could not be put on a schedule. Crawford offered a few of his men to ride with them and Jake willingly accepted. Now all Jake had to do was convince Cindy to wait here.

Cindy and Tommy came into the house, and Jake noticed she was carrying a Bible. *Did Tommy give her a Bible*, he thought. He had to admit Tommy had been a powerful influence in her life. For that matter he too, had made some changes. He looked at Cindy and felt all warm inside. *Yes*, he thought. *I certainly have made some changes.*

Jake got up from the table and walked over to them, "Hey you two, where have you been?" He said it in a joking way with a smile on his face. At that particular moment he didn't believe anyone could take her away from him.

Cindy looked at him and smiled, "Just for a walk," she said.

Jake looked at the Bible and said, "Looks like more than a walk to me."

"Well, maybe it was a little more than a walk," she said.

"Speaking of walks," Jake said, "want to take one with me?"

She smiled. "Always," she said.

They walked outside and Jake led her to the swing that was hanging there. They both sat down and Jake began. "Cindy, those guys that we're after are up near Chickasha, where we're headed. It could be dangerous because we don't know where they are. I don't feel good about taking you into Chickasha yet, and I was hoping that you would continue to stay here with Mr. Crawford."

She said nothing, but had a vacant look in her eyes as though she was in deep thought.

Jake continued, "It's the last thing in the world that I want to do, but I want you safe."

"I want you safe too," she said. "Is it really necessary for you and Tommy to go after these men? I mean the sheriff and the Cavalry are after them, and eventually they will catch them. Why not just let them do their job?"

"It isn't that simple Cindy. No matter who goes after them there's a chance they could be killed. Nothing in life is certain all we can hope for is to do our best. I don't want somebody else hurt because I didn't do my part. And what about Tommy, you know if I don't go, he'll go by himself. I have to go."

"Then, I want to go with you. You said that once you got here we would never part again."

"I think, I said that once we got these guys, we would never be apart again. But, I'm not telling you that you can't go. If you want to go it will be your decision. I would just rather you wait here. I don't want to be worrying about you."

She thought for a few minutes and then said, "How far is Chickasha from here?"

"It's just a few days ride. I could be there and check everything out and be back here in a week."

She hated to be without him again, but she understood what he was trying to do, and she really admired him for that. If he was good at anything, it was keeping his word. "Okay," she said. "I'll wait here for you, but I hope it is the last time."

"Thanks sweetheart," he said.

She melted at his words. *Sweetheart, that was even better than honey*, she thought.

Chapter 13

Eduardo and his men bypassed Chickasha, and headed straight for the old Wade farm. He was surprised to find it still vacant. He looked at the spot where he had killed the farmer and his wife. *He was a brave man*, he thought, *but not very smart or he might have lived. His wife too was not smart; she should not have run at him like that.*

He and his men set up residence there for the time being. They would need to decide what to do about getting some money and having a little fun. Tomorrow they would have to look around and see what farms there were in the area, and then make a trip into Chickasha.

The sheriff of Chickasha was Brady Smith. He was of medium build and height and a God fearing man, as well as a good sheriff. Chickasha, wasn't a very big town, it was made up of only about ten businesses. At any given time there were only about two hundred people in town including the ones that lived there: that included the families of the owners. The sheriff made his rounds of the town only twice a day, since there usually wasn't any trouble.

It was about noon, and Sheriff Brady was making his way down to Roxie's dinner for lunch, when he spotted Mr. McGregor coming out of the general store. He walked over to say hello, and then saw Joelle, McGregor's wife, as well as Molly, and Billy.

"Hi Bill," said the sheriff to Mr. McGregor. "I see you brought the whole family to town this morning."

"Yea," said Mr. McGregor. "We needed some supplies and thought we might take a break from the work, and come into town together. As a matter of fact, we thought we'd go down to Roxie's for lunch."

"That's always a good idea. She's probably one of the best cooks in town. I can never wait for our fall festivals when she brings some of her great pies."

"She always has pie," said McGregor.

"Yea, that's true, but at the festival there almost free." They all laughed.

Sheriff Brady looked at Molly. *She sure is a pretty young lady,* he thought. *She'll be a great catch for some lucky fella.* "Molly, you get prettier every time I see you. How old are you now?"

"I just turned fifteen Sheriff," She said.

"Good for you," he said. Then he remembered that she had been sweet on that Wade boy. "That reminds me Bill, have you heard anything from Tommy or his Uncle?"

"No," said McGregor. "They've been gone about at year now. They should be home soon, I would think."

Molly chimed in, "It's been thirteen months sheriff," she belted out and then felt embarrassed. She could feel her face getting red, so she quickly replied, "at least I'm pretty sure."

Everyone laughed.

Molly began thinking of Tommy again. It seems that's all she's done for the past year. Her prayers had become almost monotonous, as she continued to pray for him, every day. But she wouldn't quit. She missed him so much ever since their last few times together. *Hurry home Tommy*, she thought.

The sheriff continued, "I was just on my way down to Roxie's for lunch, if you folks don't mind joining me, it would be my pleasure."

The family looked from one to the other and then they all nodded, "Thanks Sheriff," said McGregor. "We'd be happy too, as soon as we load these supplies."

"Great," said the sheriff, "and I'll give you a hand."

They loaded the farm supplies into the wagon, and then they all walked down the street to Roxie's.

Jake and Tommy along with three of Crawford's men, left early that morning on their way home. Jake had kissed Cindy goodbye, and told her he would be back as soon as possible. They expected to be at the McGregor's place early the next morning.

Eduardo and his men had come into town that morning. They had passed the McGregor farm and found no one at home. They would have helped themselves to whatever they wanted, but decided to wait until the family was home. It was more fun that way. After all, they thought, who wants to just steal when you can have so much fun taking. So they had ridden on into town. They came in early and hitched their horses to the rail, at the back of the saloon. They made their way inside and ordered some whiskey.

Eduardo stood at the window, whiskey in hand, looking across the street at the general store. He saw the sheriff talking to a family in front of the store. *She's a little doll of a Señorita*, he thought as he looked at Molly. He looked up and down the street at what was there and then had one of his great brainstorms. Why worry about a farm when they could take this whole city? All they needed to do was to get rid of the sheriff and scare the daylights out of everyone else; then town would be theirs. Once they took over the town they could take anything they wanted from the store, the bank, and the people, and maybe even that little señorita. That wouldn't be hard to do since terror was his middle name.

He turned around and said to his four men, "Señor's grab your drinks and let us sit over here," he said as he pointed to a table. He waited for all to sit down, and then he explained his plan to them. They all began to laugh, and shake their heads, yes, as they all said, "Si, Si Señor!"

Eduardo needed to draw the sheriff into the saloon, so he stood up, and told Manuel to get over by the swinging doors. Manuel knew what he wanted, and moved over against the wall along side of the swinging doors. Eduardo walked over to the bar. He looked around the saloon and saw only about eight or ten people, *perfect*, he thought.

He turned and drew his gun, fired four shots into the whiskey bottles lined up on a shelf in back of the bar. He pointed his gun at the bartender and said, "Okay Señor, I'll take the gun that you have behind the bar." His menacing look made the bartender move faster. He handed Eduardo his double barreled shotgun. Eduardo laid the shotgun on the bar as the bartender moved further back. He turned to the men in the bar, with his gun in his hand, and motioned them to their feet and over to the wall. They all stood up with their hands held by their chests and backed up against the wall. "Drop your guns," Eduardo said.

The men looked at his three men who also had their guns drawn and pointing at them. They knew they had no choice. This was a job for the sheriff not for them. They obeyed.

Then Eduardo turned and fired the last two bullets from his revolver through the plate glass window in front, shattering it to pieces. He smiled at his men and glanced one more time at Manuel. *That should bring the sheriff running to see what was happening,* he thought. He slowly began to load his revolver and then slip it back into the holster. He leaned on the bar by the shotgun and waited with his eyes on the swinging doors.

"He is coming Eduardo," said Diego while looking out the broken window. Diego quickly walked over to the wall across from Eduardo. He kept his eyes on all of the men who were standing by the wall. This was now between Eduardo, the sheriff and Manuel.

The swinging doors opened and Sheriff Brady stood there holding each of the doors. "What's going on in here," he said as he glanced around the room. He saw the men standing by the wall with their guns on the floor. He saw Diego, and Santiago, but he didn't see Manuel behind the right door. Manuel had his gun drawn and was pointing it against the door at Sheriff Brady's side.

Sheriff Brady stood their taking in the scene. He had his attention on Eduardo who was leaning against the bar. He could see the bartender's shotgun laying there. Santeago was near the rear of the Saloon. *This doesn't look good,* he thought. *One against three is never a good choice and the shotgun was a scary thought.* He knew they could see his badge so they knew he was the sheriff. "All right hombres," he said. "What was all of the shooting about?"

Eduardo had a, 'I feel sorry for you sheriff,' grin on his face, "Hey, sheriff we were just having a little fun, Si. We don't mean any harm." Eduardo would take his time and make the sheriff sweat before he killed him.

The sheriff trying to be brave or else bluffing for effect said "Looks to me like you shot some of those whiskey bottles, and the front window. You're gonna have to pay for the damage." The sheriff knew they wouldn't pay for anything. He had seen these kind before, and he was wondering how they got into town without him seeing them. Then he took another look at Eduardo. He was all dressed in black. He glanced around the room one more time, they were all Mexicans. He remembered the Wades as his heart sank to his feet.

He quickly went for his gun only to be shot in the side though the door on his right. Wincing in pain he stumbled forward still trying to get his gun free of its holster. The last thing he saw was that silly grin on Eduardo's face as he pulled the trigger on that shotgun. The blast drove him back through the swinging doors and out into the street. He was dead before he hit the ground.

Eduardo and his men herded the men in the bar out into the middle of the street. He fired his gun into the air and began to holler for everyone to come outside and stand in the street, or he would start shooting the men from the saloon. Then he said, "As you come out throw your guns into the street. If anyone fires a shot at us, we will kill everyone. Slowly, the people began to come outside standing at first on the porch in front of the store, the bank or where they lived. They had tossed their guns into the street, but they were still standing on the porches. Then he told them one more time to come into the center of the street. Slowly, they complied.

At Roxie's, Molly had started to run outside when she heard the shots fired but Sheriff Brady had pulled her inside and told her to stay there. Then he went out the door and up the street to the saloon.

Her parents and brother were still inside Roxie's. The others had started to file out when Eduardo fired his gun from the street. The sight of the dead body of Sheriff Brady horrified everyone.

Molly's parents knew they were going to have to go outside too. They told Molly and Billy to find a good place to hide upstairs. At first they refused and their parents scolded them for not obeying them and told them what could happen to them. They were both trembling and afraid of what might happen to their parents but Molly and Billy reluctantly went upstairs to hide. They had seen Eduardo through the window and he was all dressed in black, they believed he could be the one that had killed Tommy's parents. If he was, what hope was there now that the sheriff was dead?

Molly and Billy found a good place to hide in an upper bedroom. There was a ladder fixed against a wall that led to the roof. If she and Billy needed to escape they could go up on the roof. Molly was wondering where Tommy was. He was out looking for these men and they were here. How could she get word to him when she didn't know where he was? She began to pray, *God, I know you know where my Tommy is. Please lead him and his Uncle Jake here and give them the strength and knowledge to help us.*

Jake and the others were half way to Chickasha. They had been riding harder than usual when suddenly Tommy was moved by a sudden thought. He quickly got up alongside of Jake and said, "Jake, I just got a bad feeling. I think we need to go straight to Chickasha instead of going to the McGregor's."

As Jake galloped forward he said, "Why?"

"I don't know. But I got a bad feeling that something is dreadfully wrong in Chickasha. If I'm wrong we'd only be an hour from the McGregor's."

Jake looked at Tommy and thought, *this kid is something else. First he talks to Cindy about God and changes her life. Then because she came with us on the trail Cindy and me got together. I would never have known her if Tommy hadn't talked to her. And now he gets a feeling that we should go to Chickasha. I remember his dad used to have feelings like that.*

"Okay," said Jake. Then he hollered loud enough for everyone to hear, **"We go to Chickasha."**

Chapter 14

duardo had all of the town's people in the center to the street, but he knew there would be some that didn't come out. They were either afraid or they wanted to hide out until help came. He really didn't care because he knew as they searched the stores and building's that if they saw anybody they would kill them. This is the way he would play the game.

But what would he do with all of these people? He figured there were about one hundred people and he couldn't let them stand in the center of the street forever: then too, that was too many people for four men to guard. Plus, they need to ransack the build-ings. *Where do we put these people,* he thought? The jail is too small. The saloon would work but it would be too hard to guard them there. He could kill them all but he really didn't want to do that unless he had no choice.

Finally he said, "Manuel, go to the general store and get some rope, much rope."

Manuel said, "Si" and left to get the rope.

When he returned Eduardo had the women of the town tie up everybody to each other, about six or eight people together. They were placed on the porches so that they would be easier to watch. The whole process took them several hours and finally everyone was secure. He and his men went around and tightened the ropes securely on each person. They each picked out a young woman and took them to the saloon; there they were tied up and left for later. Once this was done Eduardo told his men to gather whatever they wanted. The town was theirs.

Then Eduardo yelled as loud as he could, "If there are any others that are hiding inside and we find you, you will be killed. If you hear me you better come out now."

No sooner did he finish speaking than about ten or twelve others came out. They had been waiting to see if he would start shooting the other, when he didn't they figured they would be safer outside tied up and waiting for help then inside to get killed. As soon as they were outside Eduardo had his men tie them up.

Molly and Billy were still hiding in that upper bedroom over Roxie's Diner. They looked at each other and out the window at the man doing all the talking. They were glad that the windows were covered with lace curtains; this way they could look out but it would be hard to see in from the street.

"What do you think we should do?" Bill asked.

Molly shook her head, "I don't know Billy; but I'm concerned about those women they took over there to that Saloon. They were pretty young and I think that's where I might end up if I go out." She thought a bit more and said, "You might want to go out. I think they will just tie you up with the rest of the folks."

Billy shook his head no and said, "If you're staying here then I'm staying here." He continued, "Anyway, I found this gun in that chest of drawers over there. If they come up here for us I might get one or two of them."

Molly looked at the gun and remembered her brother was a pretty good shot. He and pa had gone hunting a lot. "Okay Billy," she said, "But no shooting unless we have no other choice, all right?"

"All right," said Billy. He placed the gun back in his belt. *It was his responsibility now to protect his sister,* he thought.

For the next several hours Eduardo's men searched out every building and ransacked them. When they came into Roxie's they had brought her back with them to fix their meals. Molly and Billy had seen them coming and went up on the roof as quietly as they could. They heard the men in the bedroom downstairs but they never came up or looked out on the roof. They were safe for now.

Latter the men came back to the diner to eat. After some time everyone could hear Roxie scream, "No, no, get off of me you filthy animals. She kept screaming over and over again until all they could hear was sobbing. Molly was afraid of what she thought had happened but she said nothing to Billy, they just looked at each other with a sad expression. There was nothing either one of them could do. Molly had prayed the whole time for Roxie but it didn't change the outcome. *Where is God when you need him the most*, she thought? *How could he let something like this happen?*

The men left the diner. They were pushing Roxie in front of them. She looked a disheveled mess; they tied her up with some other people on one of the porches and then headed for the saloon.

For hours they could hear the young women in the saloon crying and moaning. Some were heard pleading with their captors but to no avail. The people outside were praying that God would intervene. Where was he? They were thinking. They tried desperately to remove their ropes and get untied but the knots were too tight. Who would deliver them from these evil men?

No one knew what time it was when the noise of the women crying and the laughter of the men stopped. They only knew it was early morning: the sun was beginning to rise.

Jake, Tommy and the three men that came with them stopped on a ridge just outside of town. There was a feeling of 'somethings wrong' that all of them could feel. They sat there on their horses looking the town over. The sun was coming up and they could see the forms and shapes of people sitting on the porches all the way up the street. They looked at each other with their mouths open but no one spoke. They realized that the people were all tied to each other.

Then Tommy noticed the shape of someone on one of the roofs. *Who would be up on a roof?* He thought. Then he saw the figure move and lightly tapped Jake on the shoulder and pointed. The figure of a young woman stood up and was looking at them. She began to wave and point down at the street. Tommy knew it was Molly. *But what was she doing up on the roof,* he thought?

Jake spoke first, "Tommy you and Luke go that way," he pointed at the rear of the buildings to the left, "see if you can reach Molly and that looks like her brother too. We'll go this way," he pointed to the right, "I think the Mexicans have the town and they're probably in the saloon. We'll see if we can get the drop on them, it's still early and they may be asleep. Be quite son, we don't want to wake anyone up not even the people on those porches," he pointed.

Tommy nodded his head yes, and he and Luke tied up their horses to proceed on foot. The rest of the men did the same. Tommy hated to miss the action at the saloon. His first thought was that Molly and Billy would be safe where they were. He could get them after they got the Mexicans. But he couldn't wait to see Molly, and he knew she must be scared to death. Anyway, he wanted to make sure she was with him so he could protect her. He and Luke made tracks as fast and as quietly as they could.

Jake and the two men with him crept quietly behind the buildings to the saloon. Jake stood on his toes and looked into a side window. He couldn't believe his eyes. There were about three or four young women in various forms of undress: three men, he counted, were lying between them still asleep. He looked around the room for the man in black. He wasn't there. *He must be upstairs in one of the bedrooms,* he thought.

He squatted down and motioned to the other two men with him to get closer. They moved in and he began to whisper to them, "They're three of the Mexicans sleeping on the floor between several women; they probably violated them last night. Eduardo isn't with them. He's most likely upstairs. I'm going to climb up and go through one of those windows I'll motion to you from there when I locate him. Then you two will need to go in quietly with guns in hand. Try to get close enough to smack them unconscious with your guns. If that doesn't work don't take any chances. Kill them all. Don't miss and try not to hit any of the women.

Jake climbed up the railing to the roof of the porch then walked quietly to one of the windows. He looked inside. No one was there. He tried the window and it opened. He stepped inside and tip toed to the door. He slowly opened the door and looked outside. The doors were all open but one that's where he thought Eduardo would be. He figured out which window that would be and slowly walked around the roof till he got to that window. He cautiously looked inside and saw a couple lying in bed. Then he crept over to the edge of the porch and motioned the men below. They both nodded their heads and started for the back door.

Inside, Eduardo was just waking up and noticed a shadow at the window. He reached for his gun, which was beside the bed, and turned to look back at the window.

Below, the two men that came with Jake crept in the back door. There were a couple of women that were awake and they motioned to them to be quiet. Slowly they crept up to two of the Mexicans who were lying between the women. They turned their guns around and held them by the barrel as they stuck each of the men several times in the head with the handles. They wanted to make sure they were out. The third man must have heard the noise and began to rise up, and turnaround, he was struck by two bullets at the same time, and fell sideways dead. The women quickly jumped up and grabbed what clothing they could and scrambled out the front door.

Eduardo heard the gunfire downstairs and turned to look out the window at a shadowy figure. He fired twice and saw the figure go backwards and roll off the roof. He jumped up and went to the window. No one was there. Whoever it was he had shot him. He pushed the girl, who was getting up, back into bed and told her to stay there.

He quickly went to the door and quietly opened it. He stepped out onto the landing and saw two men below. They both looked up and spotted him at the same time. Both men began to raise their guns to fire but never had a chance. Eduardo fired twice and both men dropped to the floor dead.

He looked down again and saw that Manuel had been shot. He looked dead. Maybe Diego and Santiago were too since neither were moving. He walked down the steps while keeping his eyes on the doorways and looking around the room. He walked over to Diego he was unconscious from a blow to the head. He had a gaping wound in his forehead. Santiago was dead from the blows he had received. From the looks of Diego he would be asleep for a long while. Eduardo knew he was alone. He went out the back door to see who the man was he had shot on the roof. There was no one there. But there was a trail of blood leading away from the building down the alley toward the end of town. He followed the trail. Whoever it was he would kill them for what they had done. No one comes after him and lives.

The first bullet had missed Jake but the second one got him in the left side. The fall off the roof didn't help, but he knew he had to move or be killed. He got up and started to go in the back door when he saw both of his men get shot from above. *Damn that Mexican*, he thought. *The guy has nine lives.*

Jake could go inside and confront him or he could lead Eduardo to where he would have the advantage. That was the plan. Jake turned and headed down the alley to the end of town. He was limping as fast as he could to the end of the street. He saw a dark hallway and stepped inside. He put his back against a door and looked up the alley. Then he saw the trail of blood he had left. *Oh no*, he thought, *it leads right to where I am. No time to move now. I hear him coming.*

Jake slid down the door and lay across the hallway. He wanted to get as low as he could. The hope was that Eduardo would shoot over his head. He saw Eduardo come around the corner but he stopped and leaned against the building. *Hard target*, thought Jake.

Eduardo looked down and saw the trail of blood led to that hallway. He quickly ran across the Alley way to the same wall as the hallway where Jake was hiding. Jake could no longer see him. His plan was in jeopardy. What should he do now?

Up on the rooftop of Roxie's Diner was Tommy who heard the gunfire and saw Jake go into a hallway across the street. He watched and then saw Eduardo who quickly ran to the wall. Tommy knew that Jake was in serious trouble. *What should I do*, he thought? It was too late to go down to the street. He had to do something now. Then it came to him. If he used his Colt 45 long barrel he might be able to hit Eduardo, but that was a one in a million chance at this distance. However, he had no choice. Even if he missed it would draw Eduardo's attention to him and maybe give Jake a fighting chance.

Tommy lay down on the roof and took careful aim. All he could see of Eduardo was a dark image along the wall. Tommy began to pray, *God if you will, guide this bullet to its target just as you guided David's stone to hit Goliath.*

Eduardo slowly slid along the wall toward the hallway where he knew Jake was. *This gringo is about to die,* he thought.

Jake could hear nothing and the throbbing in his side was very painful but he listened intently.

Tommy took careful aim and squeezed the trigger.

Eduardo heard the shot and felt the bullet whiz by his shoulder. *Who was that,* he thought? *It didn't come from the hallway. Where did it come from?* He leaned forward stepping out from the wall and looked up. He saw Tommy lying on the roof. Kneeling beside him was another man holding a Henry rifle. He saw the flash of the gun and felt the pain as the bullet hit him in the leg. He fell back against the wall gritting his teeth. *How foolish of me,* he thought. *I thought there was only one left but there's two more up there. How many more are there? I need to get away.* It was the last thought he would have.

Jake was lying on the hallway floor when he heard the gunshot and Eduardo moan. He knew Eduardo had been hit. He took a deep breath and said to himself, *it's now or never.* Then he rolled out of the hallway into the alley about two turns and stopped. He pointed his gun in the direction of Eduardo. There was a surprised look on Eduardo's face as Jake fanned his revolver and emptied his gun into the target. Eduardo spun around and around as the bullets hammered into him he took several steps backward and turned around and looked at Jake, then fell on the ground. Jake got up and walked over to him as he reloaded his gun. He kicked him several times then knelt down and checked for a sign of breath. He was dead.

Jake turned around and looked up on the roof of Roxie's Diner and waved to Tommy and the others. They all stood up and were waving back to him.

Chapter 15

S everal weeks had passed since the Chickasha incident; at least that's what the people were calling it. They had a funeral for the sheriff and buried him with honor. Since Tommy's father was the pastor of the town and they had no other, they asked Tommy to speak at the funeral. Everyone thought he sounded a lot like his father; that made him feel very good.

As for the outlaws Eduardo and his three hombres: Diego had died from the head wound: he never regained consciousness. All four were buried outside of town in a desolate place where no one would go and they had no markers for headstones. No one would forget them but no one wanted to remember them either.

The four women that were abused by the outlaws would suffer a long time because of their ordeal. There was no psychiatrist or psychologist at that time the only one who could give them the counseling that was needed was a pastor. But there wasn't any in Chickasha.

Luke, the only man that was left of Mr. Crawford's men had returned to the Handlebar Ranch. He had taken his two dead friends with him. After the burial service Mr. Crawford sent Cindy up to Chickasha with several of his men. He sent word that if Jake or Tommy needed anything they could call on him anytime.

Jake and Cindy were very much in love. They both thought of the possibility of marriage but were a little uneasy about what life on the trail would mean. The Mayor came to Jake with an answer to their question.

"Jake I need to talk with you," he said. "The town council sent me to offer you the job of being sheriff of Chickasha. It only pays twenty dollars a month but there's room and board that goes with it. I know we're not a big city but we are growing and we could sure use your help."

"I don't know Mayor," said Jake as he looked a Cindy. "You know that people are always looking for me because of my past. I usually keep on the move because I don't want anyone else to suffer because of me, but thanks for the offer."

"Listen Jake," the mayor continued. "Mr. McGregor is on the town council and he put your name up for the position. He told us all about you, about your serving time in prison and about you being a man that lives by the gun. Right now we need a man who lives by the gun. We all saw firsthand what four outlaws could to do to our town and we need someone who is not only good with a gun but is wise enough to stay alive. We believe you are the man. And as far as people looking for you, I believe as soon as word gets out that you are the sheriff that most people will think twice about shooting a law man. I think it will give you and Cindy a place to live and maybe raise a few kids. What do you think?"

Jake looked at Cindy whose face was beaming as she gave him the 'please say yes' look. "You believe the people of this town will accept me and Cindy?"

"I wouldn't be here if I didn't."

Jake looked again at Cindy and thought, *it would be nice to have a place of my own. It certainly would be better than living on the trail like I've been doing. Plus, I think Cindy needs a place to call home and I'd love to give her that place.* "Well Mayor, I think the answer is yes."

Cindy grabbed him and hugged him as she said, "Mayor, I think Jake will be the best sheriff this town has ever had."

And so, Jake became the sheriff of Chickasha, Oklahoma: and thanks to Cindy, Tommy and God; the lonely man would not be lonely anymore.

As for Tommy and Molly, Tommy went to live with the McGregor's for a while. He had felt the call of God on his life and believed he would go to school to study for the ministry. He wasn't sure if there was a bible school anywhere near. His father had never gone to study for the ministry he just started to preach.

Maybe he would do the same thing. He had learned to trust in God, but he was still learning to forgive.

Molly only knew she was in love and wherever Tommy wanted to go she wanted to go with him. She offered to go to Oklahoma City with him and study to be a teacher. They thought that was something since his ma was a teacher and his pa was a pastor. They were excited. Should they get married now or wait. Could they wait? We'll see!

As for Tommy his mind went back to the night when Eduardo was killed. He wanted to get a clear picture of what had happened. It was amazing, he thought. He had prayed that God would direct his bullet to its target expecting it to hit Eduardo but it missed. However, it caused Eduardo to come out in the open where Luke could get a clear shot at him and Jake could finish him off. He guessed it wasn't God's intention for him to kill this man. *Will he ever understand how God works? Will any of us ever understand how God works?*

Tommy believed that if God was really calling him into the ministry then he needed answers to these questions. *Where was God in all of this*, he thought. In order to get some kind of explanation he would have to reflect back on all of the events. He had to go back to his father and mother's death.

His father and mother were real care givers for the community and were loved by everyone. If God was really in control of everything, as his father believed, then he could have protected them; but He didn't. Why? Why would God allow anything to happen to them? Perhaps the answer to those questions cannot be answered by just looking at his mother and father but by looking at what had happened over this past year or so.

It is almost certain that he would not have the relationship with Uncle Jake that he had today if this had not happened. Uncle Jake was the black sheep in the family that his parents never talked about. He wondered about what kind of relationship his father had with his uncle. This he would never know now unless Uncle Jake told him.

Then there was Cindy. If Tommy had not talked to her in that saloon and brought her with him and Uncle Jake, Jake would never have met her. After all he was in the same saloon as Tommy and he never even noticed her. Cindy may have spent the rest of her life in that saloon unless God sent someone else to talk to her. She would have never met Uncle Jake and he would have remained a lonely saddle rover going from town to town. So part of these questions may be answered in the change in Uncle Jake and Cindy's lives. Uncle Jake was now the sheriff of Chickasha and he and Cindy would be married and they could settle down together. One thing is for sure, Cindy has a relationship with God now that she had only thought could happen.

Tommy was reminded of a verse of scripture his father used to quote often, *"and we know that all things work together for good to those who love God, to those who are the called according to His purpose."* (Romans 8:28) Tommy remembered his father's words; "this didn't mean that God would make everything good in your life, but it means that he will use every event in your life for His good purpose. That out of even the bad things that happen God would make good things happen around you. What happens to you may not be good but God will use it to make good things happen. Many martyrs have died for Christ' sake but Christianity continues on."

Then Tommy began to reflect upon his own life as he began to think of all that had transpired.

I had only one thought in mind after I saw my mother and father killed, that was to kill the men that killed them. I had a quest. Along the way God had gotten a hold of my life and I couldn't quite figure it out. I remembered my conversation with God in the church and how I was so angry. I stormed out of the church vowing to never serve God and I certainly didn't want to talk to the God who allowed my mother and father to be killed.

I remembered my anger as I sat at that table in the saloon and then my conversation with Cindy. I didn't want to talk to her about God but I couldn't stop. Every time I opened my mouth someone else was talking through me. I tried not to speak but I was compelled to help her. Out of that whole conversation with her, God was changing my heart; the anger was leaving and God used me to change Cindy's life.

Tears began to flow down Tommy's cheeks as he thought about that change. Now he knows why his father served God and why he would too. He will never know what happened to all those lives that were devastated by the outlaws or to the people who cared for them. But he did know that God is a loving God, he could see that in the life of Uncle Jake and Cindy. He could see it in the McGregor's and certainly in Molly.

We live in a beautiful world that is marvelous to behold. It is filled with wonderful people of every nationality and culture; but in this beautiful world there are evil people. It is good to know that in this world there is a God who loves us and will eventually call all evil to an end. That's what I want to help God bring about, he thought. *Help me God to be a blessing to other people and use me for your glory, Amen.*

THE END